After leaving the Outcast pack, Clay Anderson and Damian Macoon are heading to Alabama where they've both secured a job with the construction company that employs Damian. Their new relationship is off to a good but not too harmonious start in no small part due to Clay still holding a grudge against Damian for turning him into a werewolf. So when they walk into the office trailer parked on the job site and Clay realizes that their boss is none other than Damian's fated mate, things get even more tense between the two.

Billy Ray Hicks was raised believing he was going to find his mate and be a cherished member of whatever pack he ended up in, but those dreams came crashing down when his bonded mate ran away and disappeared from his life before the mate bond was completed. Billy Ray always figured he'd run into Damian again but never suspected his mate would have a boyfriend when he did.

With tensions mounting between Clay and Damian, Billy Ray becomes the focal point of their ire. Damian ends up in the middle of two men—one he wants and one he needs— who both want him. Now he needs to convince them that they all belong together before he loses both.

TROUBLE'S ON THE WAY

Outcasts, Book Two

CL Mustafic

A NineStar Press Publication

Published by NineStar Press
P.O. Box 91792,
Albuquerque, New Mexico, 87199 USA.
www.ninestarpress.com

Trouble's on the Way

Printed in the USA
First Edition
August, 2018

Print ISBN: 978-1-949340-58-7

Also available in eBook, ISBN: 978-1-949340-54-9

Warning: This book contains sexually explicit content, which may only be suitable for mature readers, depictions of attempted rape and cheating.

To Mrs. Jetvig and Mrs. Richmond, my middle and high school English teachers, who taught me things like the difference between lent and borrowed but neglected to teach me where to put the commas. I forgive you.

Chapter One

CLAY

Almost nine hours of sitting in the pickup with Damian gave me plenty of time to think. Part of me thought going with him to Alabama was an okay idea. Sure the money would probably be decent, and since I was no longer gainfully employed, what did I have to lose? Another part of me thought I was crazy for not only shacking up with the guy who'd turned me into a werewolf, but now I was letting him drag me halfway across the country. Maybe contracting lycanthropy had messed up my ability to make a good decision.

I glanced over at Damian, who was concentrating on the road signs because he was looking for the exit just outside Iowa City that would lead us to one of the campgrounds. I couldn't lie to myself enough to pretend I wasn't attracted to him. Hell, who didn't have a fantasy about the tattooed bad boy? Reminding myself Damian wasn't the stereotypical bad boy, I tore my eyes off him before he could feel me staring. I spotted the exit we were looking for, but before I could point it out, Damian switched lanes and pulled off the interstate.

"You sure you don't want to drive? We could make it to Tuscaloosa by morning and sleep the day away," Damian asked for the millionth time.

"I told you I don't want to drive this rig and I'm tired anyways." I'd dozed some but not enough to stay awake and drive all night. Plus, I wasn't confident about my ability to drive the pickup with a thirty-five-foot trailer attached to it.

"You'd only have to drive for about four hours, and then I'd be fresh enough to take over, but if you're too scared to drive, I'm fine with that." A grin tugged at the corner of his lip at his dig, but all I had to do was let a growl rumble up out of my chest to kill his urge to smile.

Pulling up to the campground's reception building, Damian got out of the truck and stretched before turning back to me. "I'll go pay for the night. You want to run into the store and maybe get us some snacks and beer?"

"Sure. You want anything special?" I opened my own door but waited for his response instead of getting out.

"Maybe some ice cream, chocolate, oh, and some nachos and gummy worms."

"Are you pregnant?" I snorted and shook my head at his request as I dropped down to the ground from the pickup.

"You know those are just stories, right?" Damian called over the hood of the pickup at me.

"Hey, I have no idea what to believe anymore. I used to think werewolves were just stories." I made air quotes around "just stories" to get my point across, making him roll his eyes at me.

"Go get me my junk food." Turning, Damian went to pay for our stay while I went into the little convenience store.

The woman behind the counter watched my every move as I loaded down the little red basket with Damian's requested junk food and then grabbed a case of beer to go with it. She rang up the sale but before she was done, Damian came in the door. Her eyes widened and I could smell the change in the atmosphere around her. Apparently, she also liked bad boys, and her interest in what my beast thought of as his brought out its jealousy.

"Hey, are you buying the whole store or what?" Damian's sexy grin was at full wattage as he sauntered up to the counter. Turning it on the woman, he nodded a greeting, making her blush like a school girl.

"Not my fault your cravings are so weird." I managed to swallow the possessive warning my beast wanted to growl out at the woman. Instead, I put my arm around Damian's waist and pulled him to my side, making his smile falter. Taking it a step further when the woman's scent didn't change once she saw Damian wasn't on the market, I pointed to the row of condoms behind her. "Give me three boxes of the magnums too. I have a feeling we're going to need them tonight." I winked as Damian stiffened at my side.

"Clay–"

"Make it four." I reached down and squeezed Damian's ass. His arousal wafted up to join that of the woman's, who'd turned to get the requested condoms. She didn't make eye contact with either of us as she finished tallying the items and took my card. "Have a good night." I practically sang the words as we walked out the door.

Damian pushed away from me when we hit the parking lot. "What the fuck was that all about?" His glare would have been much more menacing if I hadn't found his mismatched eyes to be so damn alluring; plus his anger only made my beast want to make him submit to it.

"What was what all about?" I shrugged and held out the bags I was carrying in one hand. "Just getting stuff for the night."

"And what do you expect to do with twelve condoms?" His eyes narrowed as he tried to cross his arms over his chest, forgetting he was holding the case of beer, so he had to drop them back down to his sides.

He had me there. We didn't use condoms, since neither of us could catch anything, so did he think I'd intended to go out and find someone else for the night? Shit. That was not my intention, but just to see how pissed off I could make him, I decided to throw the possibility out there. "Well, maybe there will be a hot guy in the spot next to us. We should be prepared, right?"

"You're an asshole." Damian stomped off to the truck and before I could get in, he pulled away, leaving me to walk behind.

He was right. I was an asshole, but he knew that, so it was his fault for sticking around. Our spot was a bit down the road from the lodge and when I got there, Damian had already hooked up the power and was standing by the door pressing the button that pushed out the pop outs on the camper. I'd only glanced inside before we'd left so when I stepped past him, I had to stop and stare.

"Holy shit, this thing is huge." I looked over my shoulder at Damian, who was squatting to pet Stumple and Grumpkin, his cats.

"I wanted there to be enough room for both of us so we wouldn't have to be tripping over each other." Damian stood and walked across the kitchen to the living room at the end of the trailer where I was inspecting the entertainment system. "There's only one bedroom but if you want to bring someone back here, I can always sleep on one of the convertibles."

I turned to look at him because I could tell he was hurt, and though I'd wanted to keep the space between us, I didn't much like him feeling he didn't matter to me. He did mean something to me; I just wasn't sure what. I crowded him up against the wall, pressing my body to his, making his breath catch. "You'll sleep where I tell you to sleep. And if I want you in the bed with me while I'm fucking someone else, you'll lay there and watch," I growled. Where the fuck did that come from?

Damian whimpered. He knew when my beast was talking and his beast deferred to mine, always. It still boggled my mind how his huge wolf was afraid of my tiny puppy one. "I hate you sometimes, you know that?" he asked through clenched teeth.

"I know, and the feeling's mutual." I stepped back and let him go about taking care of the cats and then hooking up the water. I would have helped, but I had no idea how to do any of the things that made the camper run. I went to the bedroom on the other end of the trailer and grabbed a fresh pair of underwear before going into the bathroom and taking a shower.

When I came out of the steamy little room, Damian had changed into a pair of low-hanging sleep pants. He was curled into one of the arm chairs in the corner, watching a movie with Stumple purring on his lap and his array of snacks on a folding tray next to him. I grabbed a beer from the fridge and sat on the couch. Grumpkin jumped up and sat next to me, and after sending a look at his owner, he lay his head on my lap and started purring.

"Fuck you too," Damian mumbled to the cat before shoving a handful of gummy bears in his mouth.

"How can you eat all that shit?" I shook my head in disgust as he chased the gummies with a spoonful of ice cream.

"Fast metabolism. If I don't eat like this, I'll start looking like you." He let his eyes run over my upper body, which I'd noticed lately was getting a little scrawnier than it normally was. "I told you, the beast needs food; either you feed it or it eats away at you." He shrugged and filled his mouth with chips so his next words were interspersed with crunching noises. "Take advantage of it while you can, eat the good shit before the beast gets old and tired and then you get a pot belly."

I leaned over and grabbed a handful of his chips. "You do know you could eat something a little healthier and still keep weight on, right?" He shrugged and went back to happily munching on his treats. I couldn't get into the movie he'd started watching, so I decided maybe it was time to learn a little about the man I was living with. We did very little talking, and I knew exactly nothing about Damian beyond the things Blaine had told me, which I suspected were mostly lies. "So where are you from, exactly?"

Damian turned to me with a surprised look on his face. He swallowed and took a drink of his beer. "I'm from a tiny town outside Tuscaloosa. Why?"

"I just realized I don't know anything about you, really. I sort of figured, with that accent of yours, you were from somewhere down here, but I thought you'd stay clear of your home territory if you left your pack," I said and took a drink of my own beer. "There's not some rule against a guy like you going back to their pack's territory?" It seemed odd, but then I didn't know much about werewolf packs other than the fucked-up shit that went down at the Outcast compound. I hoped all packs weren't like that, but I wondered how bad had Damian's been for him to think Outcast was better?

"I left on my own. I'm not exiled, so though I'm sure I won't be welcomed with open arms, they won't attack me or anything. Plus, there's some treaties that have been made for weres who have to travel for work. As long as we follow the pack's treaty rules for visiting weres, we'll be fine." Damian looked uncomfortable when talking about his past, and that only made me want to dig deeper because, as he pointed out, I'm an asshole.

"So why did you leave?"

His arm stopped halfway to the tray where he was going to set his beer down. Reversing course, he chugged the rest of the can before getting up to grab another. "Do you really want to know or are you just trying to push my buttons?" He opened the new can before he got back to his chair.

"I really want to know." At first, I might have been trying to push his buttons, but now, I was curious. I'd heard pack members mention Damian having something called the mate bond. I wasn't stupid, so I figured I sort of knew what it was, but I didn't know exactly what it meant or why someone would run from it.

"I'm sure you heard what Old Ted said about the mate bond thing." I nodded, letting him know I'd heard it. "That's why I left. I didn't want it, and the only way to get out of being pressured into it was to leave."

"Was the guy that ugly?" I was trying to joke, but his face scrunched up in a sneer.

"Seriously? He was a scrawny little weakling, but that's not why I didn't want to mate with him." Damian finished his newly opened beer and got up again.

"You do know there's a bottle of vodka in the freezer." I only mentioned it because I was pretty sure he needed something stronger if he wanted to get drunk, which looked to be what he was aiming for.

"Shit, yeah, I forgot about you and your vodka." He grabbed the bottle out of the freezer and two tumblers—looked like I was getting some too. I wasn't going to complain. I took the glass he handed me and let him pour me a healthy shot. He shooed Grumpkin off the couch and sat at the other end. "It wasn't anything to do with him physically that caused me to run away, well not due to attractiveness at least. There's this huge pressure put on mated pairs and my parents were the type who were always looking to gain more status in the pack. This was their chance, and they were going to push until I accepted Billy Ray whether I liked it or not."

"Billy Ray?" I snorted out a laugh.

"Yeah, Billy Ray Hicks."

I couldn't hold my laughter, even though Damian looked serious as all get out, because man, if there was ever a hillbilly name, Billy Ray Hicks would be it.

"It's not that funny." Damian poked me in the side when I didn't stop laughing.

"Oh, it so is. Please tell me he had a mullet?"

"No, he didn't have no mullet. Shit, what the hell? Ya know we got stereotypes 'bout y'all up North too." His accent came out full force and made me grin.

"Oh yeah? Tell me one that's as funny as Billy Ray Hicks and his mullet."

"You want to hear more or you just going to laugh like a grade schooler?"

I tried to calm myself but every time I thought I'd managed it, a giggle would escape, and Damian would glare that much harder at me. Finally, I took some deep breaths and a gulp of my vodka, and that seemed to do the trick. "Okay, I'm done. So how does this mate bond work exactly? I mean, aren't you going insane from want because the bond is pulling at you or some shit?"

"You're stupid," Damian said, shaking his head at me. He sighed. "And I'm totally starting to wonder what the fuck type of shit you read."

"Fan fiction, loads of fan fiction." I snapped my mouth shut, knowing I'd just given him something personal about myself that I had never intended to share.

"Harry Potter?"

"Nah, mostly I like the comic sections, but yeah, some Harry Potter."

"Do you write it?" His smirk told me he thought the answer would be even more embarrassing than me admitting I read it, but he was wrong.

"Nope, I read. I don't write. I leave that to people who can spell. So, then what exactly does the mate bond do then? Like how do you know it's even there?" Maybe werewolves just made that shit up?

"I can feel it, but then there's also this"—he pointed at his eyes—"the way you know you'll have a bonded mate."

"Wait, so you knew all your life you'd have a mate?" I stared at his eyes, wondering how weird it was to know you had one of someone else's eyes in your head and you were fated to be with that person.

"Yeah, I knew, but I also knew that there are some, no, actually, most bonded mates never find their other half. Think about how many people there are in the world. It's amazing anyone finds their other half."

"So you grew up knowing that this guy was going to be your mate? That's fucked up."

"No, Billy Ray didn't move into our pack until he came for college. He was going to the University of Alabama. It's pretty common to have packs close to big cities, out in the middle of nowhere but in easy driving distance from a bigger town, so it's not unusual for parents with kids going out of state for college to set something up with one of the local packs. Billy Ray moved into the dorms, but he came out to the compound for the full moons. After he and I met, and by met, I mean after everyone in the pack saw his eyes and dragged me down to the café to meet him, he came out to see me. Sorta like you and Blaine."

I flinched at the mention of Blaine, who I guessed was now both mine and Damian's ex-boyfriend. "And?"

"And I could feel the bond when I got close enough to him." He shrugged and threw back what was left in his glass before filling it once more.

"I don't get it."

"Don't get what? That I didn't want to have the person I spent the rest of my life with be chosen for me? That I didn't even get along with Billy Ray all that well? That I knew I'd never be enough to protect him because god knew he wasn't going to be able to protect himself?"

"Wow."

"Things aren't as simple as just wanting to fuck someone sometimes. There's lots of things you have to think about when you're in a pack. You saw that for yourself. Pack politics can be brutal, and I know with my parents pushing, shit would have gotten bad. I'm not a strong alpha. I'm not cut out to lead, and that's what they would have expected from me," Damian said, sounding completely down on himself.

"I think you're brave." I slapped his knee as I stood up. "Knowing your limits is a good thing, and being a big enough man to act when you know shit isn't right takes guts." I held my hand out for him and he took it so I could pull him up off the couch. "Let's go fuck."

Damian nodded, his eyes lighting up when he smiled. Talking usually only got us into a fight, fucking was something we were good at doing and I didn't feel like fighting. I could take Damian's mind off what must be one hell of a mind fuck at going back to his home territory. This time, he'd have me by his side, and my beast growled at the thought of anyone trying to take what was his. Someone would die before my beast let Damian go. I was sure of it.

Chapter Two

DAMIAN

"Quit it."

"Quit what?"

"Quit humming that song or I'll pull this truck over right now." I threatened Clay but knew it would do no good. In fact, it did the opposite of what I'd intended as he started to sing the chorus of "Sweet Home Alabama" at the top of his lungs. "You sing for shit." I reached out and pinched his thigh, making him yelp and glower, but it shut him up, at least for a minute.

"I thought you said you were from Tuscaloosa." He shifted in his seat and stared out the window.

"My pack's version of the compound is west of Tuscaloosa, bordering one of the state parks. We're going north, to one of the RV parks." I turned off to take the curvy road that would lead us to the place I'd picked.

"So, you're keeping your distance then?" Clay turned to look at me, abandoning his sightseeing.

"I thought it would be best, just in case. I mean, I don't even know if Billy Ray is still here. He might have gone back to Mississippi when he graduated from college." It was true. I hadn't had contact with anyone in my pack to know if Billy Ray had hung around hoping for me to come back, and I didn't care. I wasn't the wolf for him.

"I didn't mean you were hiding from *him*. I meant the rest of the pack. You don't want to see your family or friends?"

Shrugging, I tried to think of a way to tell him I hadn't been close with my family, especially after I'd refused the mate bond—except maybe my younger brother—without sounding like a douche about it. "Most of my friends were human and my family's probably more glad than not that I'm gone."

Snorting, he shook his head. "You cause problems everywhere you go, huh?"

"What?"

"Well, you obviously had problems in your pack here and then you had problems in the Outcast pack. Sounds to me like you might be the problem." Clay rubbed his leg where I'd pinched him. "And you say I'm an asshole."

I kept my mouth shut. Clay had no idea what I'd gone through with my family or my pack before I'd left. He also had to know the shit that went down in Minnesota wasn't my fault. Hell, Pete and Willard had left me a bunch of messages trying to get me to come back and saying they'd fixed the problem. I didn't believe them. The only way they could have fixed anything is if they'd kicked out the faction of the pack who stood behind Blaine and his uncle, Old Ted, which I couldn't see them doing without a major upheaval in the system that governed them.

The RV park butted up to some prime woodland, which was just what I'd wanted. It would make the full moon phase much easier for Clay and me to manage if we had a place to run where people didn't usually venture after dark. I'd prepaid for our spot and only had to run in and sign the rental agreement and get the packet of information about the grounds from the man behind the counter. Our spot was at the very end of the park, right where I'd requested. It was the farthest from the lodge which housed the laundry room and the showers, but since our trailer was well equipped, I decided privacy was more important than the long trek to wash clothes once a week.

Once I'd parked, we got out and Clay followed me around, watching how I hooked the trailer up to the power, water, and sewer before he started complaining. "It's so fucking hot out here." He wiped his brow on the shoulder of his T-shirt.

"It's only seventy-five; that's not hot." I opened the door to the camper and both the cats twined around my legs as I stepped into the trailer. It was a bit hotter inside since I'd forgotten to switch on the AC that ran off the battery once we'd left the cooler climate behind. I went to the thermostat and switched it on.

"It's the end of February. My body can't handle this kind of heat until at least April." Clay started shedding clothes as he walked through the trailer.

"Put those back on. I need your help unhooking the truck." I picked up his shirt and tossed it at him. He groaned before throwing it on the floor, but he did button his pants back up. "I want to take you out for supper tonight, and we'll need the truck."

"Is it a date?"

"No, stupid, it's just me needing to go to the Front Porch to get me some fried catfish and hush puppies." I rolled my eyes as he followed me out, but what he asked me next actually hurt my soul.

"What are hush puppies?"

Turning on him, I stared wide-eyed at his question. "Are you serious?" He nodded. "I can't believe you don't know what hush puppies are."

"Hey, it's not a thing where I come from, so are you going to let me in on the secret?"

I walked to the fifth-wheel hitch and started the process of unhooking the pickup from the camper and he stepped in to help. "Hush puppies are cornmeal and a bunch of seasonings, and depending on where you get them, a combination of other things, deep fried. They're amazing."

Clay scratched his chin before grinning. "So it's like when my mom got sick of making corn dogs but had leftover breading, so she'd just deep fry globs of it."

"You're just trying to get me to strangle you, right?" He laughed and I knew that was exactly what he was aiming for. "You suck."

"Not as well as you." His gaze caught mine and he winked, but then I saw the shadow of his beast pass over.

Clay stood to the side while I parked the pickup in the space next to the trailer, but he didn't wait for me to get out before he grabbed me and dragged me into the camper. He was all hands as he pulled at my clothes, and since he was shirtless, I had nothing to hold on to and ended up wrapping my arms around his neck as he nipped at my lips. By the time we made it to the bed, I was wearing only my shirt. It didn't seem to bother him as he pushed his pants off and climbed on top of me to rut our hard cocks against each other.

His kisses grew in intensity as his hips moved, and this was one of the things I loved about sex with Clay—he never held back. He always had a wall up that lowered just a bit when we were fucking. I wasn't going to kid myself to think it was love that gave me a little peek into his soul, because I knew it was just his beast. His beast wanted me, even if his human mind was still undecided, and the raw animal lust took him over, giving me a lover but leaving me wanting more.

"I want your lips on my cock." The growled words came as no surprise after the teasing outside.

I flipped us over so I was on top, and Clay was staring up at me. Bending down, I kissed his lips much more tenderly than he'd ever kissed me, but before he could make it something I hadn't intended, I placed a line of kisses across his jaw and down his neck. He stretched, elongating his neck so there'd be more kisses before I moved down to his chest. I tried not to think about how much weight he'd lost as I nipped and suckled my way from one nipple to the other, but still, I made a mental note to start feeding him better.

Finding the dark line of hair, I followed it from his belly button to the top of his pubes where his scent was strongest. I buried my nose in the nest of dark curls and let my own beast wallow in the familiar aroma of our lover before I licked my way up his cock. He groaned and pressed up, trying to get me to fully take him in, but I resisted for the moment.

"Don't tease me, Damian. You don't want to make me mad."

I looked up his body to find him gazing down at me with heavy-lidded eyes, but then his kiss-puffy lips drew my attention and I whimpered. I wanted to feel his lips on my cock as much as he wanted mine on his. He seemed to know what I was thinking because he raised his hand, held up a finger, and made a twirling motion with it. I shifted on the bed and he guided my leg over his head so I was kneeling above his face.

He swallowed my cock at the same time I took his in, making me moan obscenely around the stiff flesh in my mouth, which pulled a guttural groan from him. It took willpower for me not to drill down into the soft, moist heat of his mouth. Gagging him would only make the goodness stop. I'd learned that the hard way. I let him set the pace on my cock while I tried to focus on what I was doing through the pleasure. I already knew what he liked, so I caressed his balls while concentrating on the sensitive crown of his cock.

He wasted no time. Slicking his fingers with his spit, he knew what to do to get me off, too, and all too soon I was coming down his throat. He barely let me enjoy the rippling aftereffects of my orgasm before he rolled me over and started fucking my mouth. I relaxed my jaw, giving his cock room to slide across my tongue while I pursed my lips around his length. With a growl, he let loose and I struggled to swallow around his girth until he eased slowly out of my mouth to turn and flop down next to me on the bed.

"That was good." His words were mumbled into my neck as he snuggled in and promptly fell asleep.

I stared at the ceiling for a while, not wanting to disturb Clay by getting up, and since he was wrapped around me, I would assuredly wake him if I tried. My mind was in a bit of turmoil, had been since we'd crossed into Alabama. Taking a job so near my old pack was probably one of the dumbest ideas I'd ever had, but if I was going to be honest with myself, I'd almost felt driven to come home. I hated to blame it on something as lame as the mate bond and I knew that's not how it worked, but for some reason, my beast felt the pull to this place. I looked down at the top of Clay's head, his dark hair messy as he slept peacefully on my shoulder. I had to wonder what would happen when the pack got wind of me shacking up with an infected. Nothing good, I supposed. I drifted off but my sleep was haunted by a pair of eyes, oddly like my own, but oh so different.

THE FRONT PORCH was a tiny hole-in-the-wall local place in Tuscaloosa. Clay didn't look impressed when I parked out front, but he got out and followed me in just the same. He was relaxed and in a good mood after not only sex but an afternoon nap. Once inside, his disbelieving attitude changed when the smells wafting from the kitchen hit his nose. He took the seat across from me at one of the tables by the window.

"What can I git for y'all?" The older waitress was at our table before we'd even picked up the single-sheet laminated menu.

"I'll have iced tea to start." I looked at Clay.

"Iced tea sounds good. Is it sweetened? Cause I'd like mine without sugar if it is."

Watching as the waitress opened and closed her mouth like a beached fish, I jumped in to save her from having to explain that down here, there was no such thing as unsweetened tea. "It's sweet tea. If you don't want sugar in it, you're probably better off ordering something else."

"But—"

"Clay, just order a coke."

"I'll have a coke." Clay glared at me as he said the words.

I ordered for both of us and when the waitress brought our plates, Clay watched me put tartar sauce on my fried catfish before shaking his head and taking a bit of his without. He crinkled his nose and reached for the bottle while I chuckled at him. He tentatively tasted the collard greens, which must not have excited him, but the hush puppies had the intended effect and he wolfed his down and eyed mine.

"See what you've been missing all these years?"

"They're good but, I could do without all this green stuff." He flicked a piece of greens at me with his fork.

"Stop acting like a three-year-old. Eat your veggies and I'll order you another side of hush puppies." His grin was genuine as he stuffed his biscuit in his mouth and then shoved some greens in there too. And he said I ate like a pig!

He stopped stuffing his face long enough to ask, "What time do we have to be on the job tomorrow?"

"We have to be there at seven. We'll meet with the guy running the site and he'll assign us to one of the ground teams. I'm not sure what we'll be doing because I don't usually work on the actual job," I said as I slapped his hand when he tried to steal one of my hush puppies. I motioned the waitress over and ordered a double side of them for Clay, trying not to roll my eyes when he took the opportunity to snatch one off my plate while I was distracted. "You're really being annoying today, you know that?"

He shrugged. "Must be all the grease hanging in the air. You guys eat anything that isn't deep-fried down here?" He waited for me to take the bait, but I ignored his jab at how my people ate long enough for him to give up on it and go back to asking about work. "What do you mean you don't usually work on the actual job? What do you normally do then?"

"I work... well, I head up, the closing team."

"What's that?"

"When they're done with the project, the closing team comes in and makes sure everything is cleaned up. We ship the equipment to a new site, do some dirt moving to landscape so we leave the place in a decent condition for the landowners, and just generally do all the shit the foremen don't want to do at the end."

"Sounds like a shitty job." Clay smiled at the waitress as she put a plateful of hushpuppies in front of him.

"It's not. I like it. But when I called, this was the only thing they had open where they'd hire you on too." I could have been in Oklahoma again if it wasn't for Clay needing a position too.

"You sound thrilled about that," Clay said around a mouthful of food.

"I wanted you with me, but it's not what I usually prefer to do." It was blunt, but I knew he knew my feelings for him ran deeper than his for me. He was torn between his beast wanting me and his human who could barely stand me at times, where mine were on the same page. I wanted Clay.

"You're just a glutton for punishment, you know that?"

There was nothing I could say to refute that so I just sipped my tea while he polished off the rest of his food.

"IT'S SO EARLY," Clay whined when we got in the truck. He was not a morning person and I could see that getting out of bed before sunrise every morning was going to be a struggle for him.

"You can sleep for another twenty minutes." I pulled out of the RV park and drove south toward the jobsite while Clay leaned against the door and started snoring. That man could fall asleep at the drop of a hat. Almost exactly twenty minutes later, I pulled onto the site where, against expert opinion, they were putting up ten wind towers. Everyone knew our part of the state wasn't known for its wind speeds unless we were getting bad weather, so why they were putting up wind towers was anyone's guess.

Poking Clay to wake him, I opened my door and got out to wait until he joined me at the front of the truck. I stopped to admire how good he looked in his work clothes, but then reminded myself we were there to work. "We have to go into the trailer over there and probably fill out paperwork and go over the safety shit before we start," I said as Clay and I walked to the white jobsite trailer that housed the employee break room and the project manager and foreman's offices.

"Aww, I was hoping I'd get to drive the bulldozer right away." Clay bumped my shoulder with his when I snorted.

On the stairs to the door Clay gave me a playful shove and went inside first. I grabbed the back of his shirt, prepared to hold him back so I could introduce the two of us to the guy overseeing the project since it was someone I hadn't worked with before, but then my beast stopped me in my tracks when it caught a familiar scent. The man standing beside the counter, pouring a cup of coffee turned around and my breath caught as I froze.

Chapter Three

BILLY RAY

It's not like I wasn't expecting Damian Maccon to walk back into my life at some point, and even knowing it was going to be that morning didn't stop the sight of him from hitting me like a lead fist in the gut. I tried to act casual as I turned around and took in not only my bonded mate but the guy he'd brought into the company and my trailer. It was obvious they were together by the way the dark-haired guy, Clay Anderson was the name on his employee sheet, put his hand possessively on Damian's back when he realized something was amiss. His intense gaze burned into mine and I saw the exact moment when he realized who I was, tipping me off that Damian had told him he had already met his bonded mate.

"Well, as I live and breathe, if it ain't Billy Ray Hicks!" Clay's exaggerated imitation of a Southern accent didn't quite hide the sneer lurking beneath the words. Damian elbowed him, but it didn't seem to faze the guy who took a step in my direction.

"And who might you be?" I asked, squaring my shoulders to face him. Two things I noticed about Clay right off the bat—he was a were; I could smell his beast, which had probably risen closer to the surface when it realized I might be competition for it, and he was unbelievably attractive. I found the second thing strange, because looking at him I could see he wasn't conventionally handsome; there was just something there that my beast found undeniably hot.

"Careful, Billy Ray." It was Damian who issued the growled warning at me as he stepped up to Clay's side.

My eyes dropped to my feet. I would always be submissive and no amount of muscle added to my body would make me anything else when it came to stronger pack members. "I wasn't challenging him," I mumbled. This is not how I'd planned for this to go.

"Uh...Damian?" Clay sounded unsure of what was happening, making me look up at him.

"We'll talk about it later," Damian said to Clay before addressing me. "Clay needs to sign his papers and we should get to work."

"Yeah, um, I have his paperwork on my desk and the safety videos are cued up for him in the other room. Conrad's not expecting him out on the site until after noon." I turned to go into my office and they followed.

"You're the foreman?" Damian asked, looking around my office.

"I'm actually the project manager on this one. It was supposed to be Marshall's job, but his kid fell out of a tree and broke his back, so he had to go back home." I found the stack of papers for a new hire and handed them to Clay, whose eyes followed my every move. He took the papers and I pointed to the small table set up in the corner where he could sit and fill them out.

"So you knew I was coming." Damian sat in one of the chairs in front of my desk as I walked around and took my chair.

"I did." I fiddled with the pen on my desk as I waited for him to lay into me.

"You could have warned me."

My head snapped up so I could meet his gaze, a mirror of my own staring back at me. "And just how was I supposed to do that?"

Damian sighed and crossed his leg so his ankle rested on his knee, fingers tapping against the denim of his jeans. "You have a point there, I guess."

"Listen, I don't think this is going to be a problem. I don't have too much direct contact with the ground crew. I mostly sit here in the office and answer the phone to listen to people bitch about budgets and time constraints." I wanted Damian to stick around and give me time to make him see I'd changed. I'd grown up and I wasn't the naive farm boy from Yazoo City, Mississippi, anymore.

"I hadn't planned on turning tail and running, Billy Ray." Damian glowered at me, which made me feel like I'd said something wrong, though I knew I hadn't.

"One other thing, your pack didn't file papers with ours for you and—" I used a thumb to indicate Clay—"him to run with our pack. Did you want me to ask Bubba about it?"

Damian shifted nervously in his seat before dropping his foot back to the ground. "We don't have a pack and I don't think either one of us will be welcome."

"You're both lone wolves?" This was news to me and I figured it would be to my pack too. No one kept close tabs on Damian, but we did try to keep up with his general whereabouts. Last I'd heard he was with a pack up in Minnesota. I wondered what had changed and why he was out on his own but knew it would be a mistake to ask.

"Not exactly lone wolves if we're together." Damian shrugged like it was no big deal, but his scent tipped me off to his agitation over talking about it.

"You should at least let the pack know your plans and where you'll be doing your prowling during the full moon phase, but I'm sure you'd be more than welcome back home." I knew for a fact Damian's homecoming was something most of the pack was looking forward to, but I wasn't going to tip my hand in case I needed that information later.

"I'll tell you and you can take it back to the elders. How's that sound?" Damian looked back over his shoulder at Clay, whose head was bowed over his paperwork, but I was sure he was listening as the pen scratched across the surface.

"I can do that."

"We're staying up at the RV park by Lake Lurleen. We plan to run the woods there during the full moon. We'll be out of the pack's way, and since Clay is still a pup, we won't get into any trouble." Damian stared at me, daring me to say what was on the tip of my tongue about his revealing Clay was an infected in such an offhanded way.

"I'll tell them where you'll be and that you've agreed to the visiting were treaties that cover the area," I said biting back my surprise and keeping it civil. There was no way I'd be telling the pack about Clay. I was loyal to them, but my first priority lay with my bonded mate, and if he had a reason to protect Clay, I'd have to take up that burden too.

"I'd appreciate that." Damian stood, and I followed his lead. His eyes swept my body and he shook his head. "You've changed some, Billy Ray. You look good."

His compliment made me feel really good, but Clay's head came up as he scented the air around him and a low menacing growl rose from his chest at my spike in arousal. My beast cowered as I tried to puzzle out how what I'd just thought could be possible.

"It's true," Damian said, drawing my attention back to him. "Clay doesn't even know, but I can feel him, here." Damian put his hand just under his solar plexus as he said the hushed words.

"But he's an infected human." The words fell out of my mouth like rocks, because with that gesture Damian basically told me he belonged to Clay and it felt like a hot knife had just been run through my stomach. Though it was absolute nonsense that wolves mated for life, every werewolf knew his beast could be insistent upon some things from time to time, and when your beast set its heart on a person, sometimes that was all you needed for that person to start burrowing into your human mind.

"He is." Damian nodded.

Swallowing hard, I took a moment to let what he was telling me sink in. Years of knowledge passed down from generation to generation told me it couldn't be true. "If you say so." Well, that was not exactly what I wanted to say, but again, my beast was always actively trying to avoid conflict, and telling Damian he was a damn fool wouldn't have done anything but get me beat up.

"I'm done with this. What's next?" Clay stood and walked over, eyeing the two of us like he was trying to figure out if we were going to fight or fuck and if we did fuck, would he be welcome to join in.

Sliding my gaze from Damian to Clay, I took the papers from him and said, "Next is the new-hire videos that you'll watch in the room down the hall." I took them down to the room set up with a couple of computers where we did our employee training. Setting Clay up with a video, I led Damian out of the room. We stood by the door to the trailer as he prepared to go out to find the foreman. "I'd like it if we could get together and talk sometime."

Damian rubbed the back of his neck and huffed out a breath. "I'm not sure that's a good idea, Billy Ray. I'm with Clay and—"

"I'm not asking for anything other than you meeting me for a beer or two so we can talk. You know this isn't going to go away until we do something about it." He might not want to admit it, but once we'd met and knowing my mate was someone I knew, the urge to complete the link had grown stronger. It was funny because before I'd looked into his eyes, I'd felt nothing from the bond. It wasn't like it was always on my mind, but in quiet moments it came to the surface, and I found myself wondering what Damian was doing out there in the world without me. I wondered if he ever thought about me.

"This thing isn't going to go away but doing something about it is not going to happen because I'm still not the guy for you, Billy Ray. I never was." He turned and grabbed the doorknob but paused. "I think sometimes even fate and nature can fuck up." He opened the door and then he was gone, but it didn't hurt so much, because this time I knew I'd see him again.

DRIVING HOME AFTER a completely unproductive day, I dreaded what was to come when I got there. I knew I'd have questions to answer when I arrived. One of the good things about Damian not asking about his family or the pack was that I didn't have to tell him I lived with his family in his old bedroom. The Maccons had taken me in when my own parents found out my bonded mate had run away and took his actions to mean I was lacking. Even though I'd grown up with special status within my pack, Damian's rejection made everyone forget I had once been revered. Not that I loved being revered or anything, but getting kicked out on my ass wasn't very pleasant in comparison.

As usual, when I pulled into the driveway at half-past eight, everyone else was already home. Sighing, I stared at the three-story renovated farmhouse that had been in Damian's family for seven generations. I grabbed my empty travel mug and got out. I didn't even make it all the way through the door before Linda, Damian's mom, was standing before me, giving me that look I knew so well.

"He doesn't want to run with the pack and he's with someone." I tried to step past her, but she blocked my way.

"Well, we knew he was with someone, but is he *with* someone?" Hands on her hips meant Linda wanted answers and wouldn't stop until she had them all.

"Can I at least take my boots off and maybe get something to eat while we talk about this?" I bent down to untie my boots before she could answer.

"I'll get you a plate. Fried chicken and mashed potatoes tonight."

She left me to finish stripping off my boots. I snuck down the hall and up the stairs to my bedroom where I quickly got in the shower in the attached bath before she realized I'd been gone longer than it took to remove footwear. I'd have to face her ire, but it gave me some time to calm down. I'd already decided what I was going to tell Damian's family. I just needed to pull myself together enough to do it.

Back on the main floor, I could hear Linda banging around the kitchen while David and Dante, Damian's father and brother, held a lively discussion at the table. Two pairs of green eyes, so close to the same color as my right one, turned to me when I walked into the room and sat down at the table across from Dante. My plate was already set on the table, but before I could pick up my fork, the questions started.

"So, are you going to tell us about this Clay guy or not?" David asked, shifting in his seat so he was facing me instead of Dante.

"Not much to tell." I shrugged and picked up a chicken leg to take a bite out of it.

"There's gotta be something about him you can tell us. Damian wouldn't bring the guy home if he wasn't something," Linda said, plopping down in the chair at the end of the table.

"He didn't really bring him home now, did he?" Dante glared at me. He was the only one in the family who wasn't on my side when it came to Damian. Dante had always looked up to his older brother and had taken his side when it came to rejecting me, saying if it had been him, he'd have done the same.

"He may as well have." David's steady voice was the one that usually kept the other two family members from getting at each other's throats over the wayward Maccon. "Maybe he just needs to see we're not going to run that other boy off, and he's taking it slow to see the reaction of the pack."

I dropped my chicken leg as I opened my mouth to tell David the exact opposite was true. Damian knew the fate for an infected in our pack, but I snapped my mouth shut to block the words. I wasn't going to be the one to blab Damian and Clay's secret. "I don't think he has any intention of coming back into the fold."

"Probably not now that he knows you're still here." Dante pushed back from the table—chair legs screeching across the linoleum—got up, and stomped out.

Linda put her hand over mine where it rested on the table. "I'm sure it has nothing to do with your being here, sweetie. He's always been slow to realize what's in his best interest. This Clay, is he a nice man?"

"I didn't really talk to them much, so I can't say." I looked to David whose eyes were narrowed as he studied me. He was more perceptive than his wife when it came to sussing out lies, but I knew he wouldn't push me on this yet. He was also more patient than Linda. He was willing to wait as long as it took for Damian to come and put his family back where he thought they rightfully belonged—at the top of the pack.

"I'd like you to invite Damian and Clay to meet us for dinner this weekend," David said, then quickly put his hand up to stop me when I tried to interrupt. "It doesn't have to be here on pack land. We can meet up somewhere in town, even in Birmingham, if he feels like he wants more space between him and the pack."

"We just want to see him." Linda squeezed my hand as she added her voice to the plea, making it hard for me to resist.

"I'll ask him tomorrow."

Linda hugged me and David smiled as he got up, patted my shoulder, and walked out. "Eat your supper now, before it gets cold." Linda followed her husband out of the room, leaving me to eat in peace.

I hated being caught in the middle of Damian and his parents, and knowing I was the reason Damian had left made it that much worse. I wondered sometimes if his parents hadn't pushed so hard from the first moment they'd found out we were bonded mates, if things might have turned out differently. Damian didn't want the power his parents were so hungry for and being with me would have thrust him to the head of the pack, no matter what, but maybe if he'd been given time to adjust, he'd have accepted it and me.

Scraping my leftovers into the trash, I rinsed my plate before going to my room. I opened my closet and, not finding what I was looking for, went instead to the dresser that had two sets of drawers running down the front. I pulled out the second from the top on the right and stared at the contents. Feeling more feminine than masculine, as I did at that moment, I pulled out the long, golden silk negligée and rubbed it against my cheek before taking it to the bed where I laid it out. I stripped out of my sweats and picked up the gown. Letting it drop down my body, I stood for a moment to enjoy the way it caressed my skin before I climbed into bed and settled back to watch a movie.

My mind was preoccupied and drifted off to think of Damian and Clay and what they might be doing right at that moment. I wondered if Damian let Clay in the way I'd hoped he'd let me into his life. Jealousy burned hot in my chest as I clutched my pillow and cried myself to sleep.

Chapter Four

CLAY

"How was your day?"

Turning slowly, I gave Damian my best glare, making it clear how my day had gone just before I opened the door to his truck and climbed in. "My balls are still vibrating. How do you think my day went?"

"You're lucky. You could have been stuck holding a shovel all day." He turned the key in the ignition as he chuckled at me. "Driving around with Carl all day is the easiest job you could have pulled."

"He talks all the time, never stops. I don't even think he breathes." The old Texan had talked my ear off the entire eight hours I'd sat beside him in his dump truck. The foreman asked me if I thought I could learn to drive a belly dump and pass the test quickly because they were short on site drivers and after he'd told me it paid six bucks more, I'd said, hell yeah. I didn't realize I'd be trapped in a truck with chatty Carl while he taught me the basics and then when he'd handed me the manual to study from, I'd second-guessed my decision.

"You'll survive, and if you don't, I'm sure Carl will be happy to assist in your burial." Damian grinned at me before turning his eyes back to the front, but as soon as he did, his grin turned into a frown. I stopped glaring at him and looked out to see Billy Ray climbing into a Jeep.

"You didn't tell me he was hot." I knew we'd have to talk about Billy Ray at some point, but I'd been hoping to have a few drinks first because I didn't like the irrational jealousy I felt over Damian. It still burned my ass that my beast held such sway over me when it came to him.

Damian's hands tightened on the steering wheel, turning his knuckles white from the force of his grip. "You think he's hot?"

"Duh, and you do too." Leaning over, I sniffed him. "I could smell the two of you. Surprised you didn't just jump each other in the trailer." I straightened back up and waited for him to deny it, but he didn't.

"He's put on some muscle and grown into his nose." Damian shrugged like it was nothing, but I wasn't buying it.

"If you think you want to go back to your pack, I'm not going to stop you." Even as I said the words, my beast twitched in anger in the back of my mind. *Fuck you*, I thought at the little bastard. I was the only one in control of my life.

"What makes you think I'd want to go back there? You're always thinking with your dick, and one day it's going to get you into trouble." Damian pursed his lips and stared straight ahead at the road as he drove through the dying light of twilight.

"I'm just telling you I don't expect this thing to be forever, and if you feel like you have better options elsewhere, you're free to take them."

His pursed lips turned down in a frown, but he didn't say anything to let me know what he was thinking. We were silent the rest of the way back to the RV park. It gave me time to think about Billy Ray and what my own beast had thought of the guy. I didn't much like it's reaction. My beast was a greedy bastard who thought the idea of having both Billy Ray and Damian would be a good idea. My human brain knew that was an extremely bad idea, even if my dick disagreed. I wished I could tell Damian that and prove I didn't always think with my cock, but I was afraid of his reaction if I told him I, too, wanted to fuck the hell out of little Billy Ray.

THE NEXT DAY, I realized that things would probably be okay on the job. We didn't have any business in the trailer and Damian had packed us enough food and drinks in a cooler that going into the break room wasn't necessary for us to eat. We wouldn't even have to see Billy Ray, and after a frosty evening in the camper with Damian, I was damn thankful for that—until lunch time rolled around. Damian and I were sitting on the tailgate of his pickup, our food set out between us, when Billy Ray came out of the trailer.

I watched as he stopped and looked around the parking lot, and when his eyes landed on us, I knew he'd found what he was looking for. He didn't hesitate. Instead, he looked like he put some extra purpose in his step as he strode across the packed gravel toward us. "Looks like the boss man's coming." I tried to grin, but my beast had its hackles up, making me clamp my lips shut to keep the rumbling growl inside.

"Ayup." Damian watched along with me until Billy Ray stood only a few feet in front of us.

He looked at Damian like he was the second coming but schooled his expression by the time he turned to me and nodded a greeting. "Clay, how's the job going?"

"Pretty good so far, boss." I didn't even pause in my eating. I had only so long for my break and Damian was trying to fatten me up, so I had two more sandwiches to eat before my time was up.

"Good to hear." Turning back to Damian, he didn't spend any more time pretending he was there to shoot the shit with me. "Can I have a word with you?"

"Nothing's stopping you." Damian side-eyed me as he answered.

"I meant in private."

"I don't think there's anything either of us have to say to each other that Clay can't hear."

I grinned when Billy Ray sent me a scowl. He sure did have a pretty set of eyes on him, even when they were scrunched up in hatred. I winked and blew him a kiss before remembering he was technically my boss.

He rolled his eyes but otherwise ignored me. "It's a private matter, not about the job."

"I can't think of one thing we'd have to talk about that could be considered private, Billy Ray. Whatever you have to say to me can be said in front of Clay." Damian repeated. He was like an immovable object. It was my turn to give him a look. I wondered why he was making it seem like our relationship was more than it was by declaring he was willing to discuss all private matters in front of me.

Billy Ray sighed. "Fine. Your parents would like you and Clay to meet them for dinner one day this weekend." He held up a hand to stop the automatic refusal Damian opened his mouth to deliver. "Not at the house if you don't want. They're willing to go so far as Birmingham if you'll agree to go."

"I have nothing to say to them. It would be the same old thing and do you really want to sit through another one of those kinds of dinners?"

"I kinda want to meet your parents." I couldn't let the opportunity to poke at Damian pass.

"Clay..."

"What? I want to see what sort of people produced a guy like you." I shrugged like I didn't know I was taking a potshot at him.

"We'll talk about why that's a bad idea later." Oh, he was angry! I'd managed to get under his skin in front of Billy Ray, which probably pissed him off. Having an audience to one of our little back-and-forths apparently wasn't something Damian liked. "Tell them no. I don't want to go to dinner with them. No, actually, tell them not only do I not want to go to dinner with them, I don't want to see them at all. Make it clear that if they try to show up here or at the park, it will end badly for all of us."

"Your mom really misses you and Dante is—"

"Shut up." Damian's glare was razor-sharp as he looked at Billy Ray. "Don't fucking talk about him to me." Billy Ray's mouth snapped shut and color rose on his cheeks before he looked down at his boots.

"Who's Dante?" Crumbs of food fell from my full mouth as I asked, but I didn't care; this was intriguing. Damian didn't talk about his family or the pack he'd left behind, and I was curious even if I pretended not to care.

"My little brother." Damian turned that fiery look to me, as if daring me to ask more dumb questions. "You've got my answer, so why not just go back into your air-conditioned cage and leave me alone." He was talking to Billy Ray even though his eyes never left me.

"I'll tell them." Billy Ray nodded at me before he turned to leave.

Once he was out of earshot, which was back in the trailer because wolves had hella good hearing, Damian asked, "You have any questions you think are worth me beating the crap out of you to ask?"

"Nope."

"Good."

We finished our lunch and parted ways without another word spoken between us.

TIME WENT BY fast when working twelve or fourteen hour days, and weeks were the same when the only day off was Sunday and it was spent doing laundry and shopping for food. I was relieved when the full moon phase for the month hit. I knew we had four days off and I was looking forward to it, even if I'd spend three of them in pup form.

"Can we go yet?" It was the third time I'd asked Damian if we could leave the trailer after we'd come home from work and showered, and I knew the answer before he turned and glared at me to deliver it.

"We're not leaving until you shift. There's no point to going before then and it's still light out so if you shift out in the open, someone might see you. Just eat that steak and wait." He plopped a second hot baked potato on my plate to go with my third helping of meat.

"You suck."

"I know. That's why you like me." He winked and sat on the other side of the bench seat with his own meal. We'd usually be eating outside, but it was hotter than hell and the air conditioning felt too good for us to leave any longer than it took for Damian to cook our steaks. Then it hit me. I wondered how the heat would affect me in my other form when it was this hot.

"How the hell am I going to not melt when I turn into a dog?"

Damian cocked his head and studied me like he was trying to figure out if I was really asking a sincere question or not. I stared back and waited until he sighed and answered. "How many dogs have you seen melt before?"

I shrugged.

"You'll be fine." He snorted before he went back to eating.

After taking a few more bites, I sat back. "I'm done. I can't eat another bite or I'll puke."

Damian narrowed his eyes at my plate. "You could at least finish that steak."

"It's the third one! I've eaten a pound of meat already and two potatoes." I swore he was trying to make me so fat I wouldn't be able to move, but even after eating like I was pregnant with quadruplets for two weeks, I'd barely gained any weight.

"Fine, I'll just cut it up and you can eat it after we get back from our run. Your pup is always starving after a good frolic." He finished his steak and stood, picking up both plates and taking them to the kitchen counter where he proceeded to cut my leftovers into pup-sized pieces.

"You know, it sort of freaks me out when you treat me like your pet puppy." I got up and started stripping out of my shorts and tank top because I could feel my beast niggling at the back of my brain, and I hated getting trapped in my clothes when I transformed.

"Would you rather I leave you to starve?" He put the food in a container in the fridge before raising an eyebrow at my nudity. "You going to change already?"

"I feel it and I'd rather be ready for it." I looked at the clock. The timing was never exact, but it didn't seem like it was too early. I walked over and flopped on the couch, eliciting a grunt from Damian who hated it when I sat on the furniture naked. He said it was unhygienic or some shit, but I didn't care, and he wasn't annoyed with it enough to start a fight—yet.

He tidied up the kitchen and grabbed a couple of beers, handing one to me as he passed. "Make sure you don't spill on the couch." He popped the top off his beer and clicked the television on. Using the remote, he idly flipped through the channels while I drank my beer.

"I thought the whole full moon thing was just a myth. I mean, why can't we change whenever we want?" I was just grumbling to grumble because I was bored, and Damian and I had been spending all our free time together, so he was an easy target when I wanted someone to argue with. Most of the time he didn't take the bait, but this time he rolled his eyes.

"Because that's not how it works. How many times do you have to have something explained to you before you get it through your thick skull?"

"It just seems dumb that being a werewolf is limited to three days a month."

"It's not. I could have changed yesterday and maybe even the day before that and sometimes when I get pissed off, I can change almost any time. But I have to be really fucking pissed off." He sent a glare at me as if it would warn me that I was wearing on his last nerve and he could beast out if he felt like it.

"So why is this the first I'm hearing about it?"

"Because you're infected and most likely your changes will be limited to the full moon even when you can control them." He was hiding something from me. I could tell by the way he looked away when I tried to keep eye contact with him. It was his tell, and I think he knew it because he chugged his beer and stood up. "Finish that so I can throw the bottles in the recycling bin outside."

"Tell me what you're not telling me first." I held the beer just below my lips and then moved it when he made a grab for it.

"Just finish that beer before you change and drop it on the couch or the floor."

"Why do you always try to hide shit from me?" Nothing pissed me off like his unwillingness to tell me the truth about shit I felt like I should know. It probably had something to do with how we'd ended up together, which still raised my hackles when I thought about it. Withholding information was as good as lying, in my book.

"I'm not hiding anything from you because there's no way to know for certain how someone who's infected will handle the change. There's no rule book on it, and you of all people should know that."

I had to give him that one, since I'd spent three days as a human puppy and a month as an actual puppy, when I'd somehow managed to force the change to save Damian's life. I opened my mouth to argue more, but then the world shifted as my body became smaller and a lot hairier. The only sound that came out of my mouth was a yip.

Damian made a quick grab for my beer bottle and managed to get it before it hit the floor. He grinned before bringing it to his lips and draining it. "Ah, blessed quiet at last."

I barked at him. I may not be able to say all the things I wanted, but I sure as hell didn't need to be quiet.

"Shut up or I'll sic Stumple and Grumpkin on you." Damian left to deposit the bottles in the bin outside the door of the camper while I jumped down off the couch and looked around for the cats. They wouldn't attack me, but they did like to bat at my tail, which pissed me off because the tail was mine alone to attack.

I went to watch Damian as he made sure everything was secured for the night. My butt wiggled so hard I almost fell out the door, but Damian picked me up and carried me back in the trailer just before I took a tumble.

"I know you're excited, but I have to make sure no one robs us blind while we're out for the night." He put me on the floor and then made the rounds, locking all the windows, and then he fed and watered the cats. "Okay, are you ready?" I wagged my tail and gave an affirmative bark. "Of course, you're ready."

He grabbed one of the leashes he used for the cats and came at me. We had discussed this and why it was necessary, but my puppy must have forgotten because there was no way it was letting Damian put that thing around our neck. I dodged and then ran across the room while Damian gave chase and cussed me and every relative I had, living and dead, before he cornered me. I whined as he slipped the end over my neck, and I swear the cats looked smug as they watched him lead me around on it.

"Oh, stop fussing. It's not that bad, and it's only until we get out into the woods." Damian looped the leash over the metal stair railing after we got to the ground. "You two behave until we get back." He locked the door and then grabbed the end of the leash again, but he had to tug because my tail had gotten my attention, and I was busy going around in circles. "You're too cute. Too bad you're such an ass when you're in your human form."

I growled at him, but then I knew I wasn't the most pleasant person to be around, and I took my anger out on him more often than not because he was a soft target. We walked into the woods and Damian left the trail after about half a mile. He took the leash from around my neck before stripping out of his clothes and folding them into a neat pile that he placed in the V of a tree branch. He stretched in the moonlight, and then he was a wolf.

My beast loved Damian's beast, thinking it was great fun to chase the grown wolf's tail. It was time I faced the fact that my puppy was tail obsessed. Damian was a good sport about it though and let me bite at him for a bit before he pawed me off and gave a sharp bark that my beast knew meant he wanted me to follow him. It was freeing to run through the woods in my other form, and I forgot all about the question Damian had refused to answer earlier as we splashed through the small creek and then chased a squirrel through the underbrush. Being a pup was just too much fun to let my human thoughts intrude to bring me down.

Chapter Five

DAMIAN

I could tell Clay was getting tired. Even though I wanted to keep running, I knew I needed to get him home so he could sleep. I led the pup back to where I'd disrobed, and he flopped over on his side to wait for me to change and get dressed. His little puppy snores started up before I'd even gotten my pants buttoned. After dressing, I decided not to put the leash on him and, instead, picked him up. He snuggled into my arms as I carried him back to the trailer.

The cats were happy to see me, and I had to push them aside to get into the camper. Clay woke when I set him down. He went straight for the cat's food and water bowls, a mistake that ended in me having to corral the cats, who decided to fight for what was theirs, in the bedroom.

"You know better than to try to eat their food." It had been the reason behind their first spat that left Clay pissing on the carpet in my trailer back on the compound, which I thought had taught him a lesson, but apparently not. Grabbing his leftovers from supper, I nuked them for just a second to take the chill off before adding a small can of soft puppy food and setting the bowl on the floor. Clay dug in right away, leaving me to make a sandwich for myself.

I sat at the counter and watched him. He was getting bigger; already his legs were longer, making him look more like a wolf and less like a ball of fur. He was going to be a huge mutt once he grew into his beast. I found myself wondering what sort of wolf Clay would have been if he'd been born into it rather than infected. Of course, after seeing the things I'd seen lately, I questioned everything I'd ever learned about the infecteds among us.

Clay pawed at my leg and whined to get my attention. "Hold on, just let me finish my sandwich and we'll hit the sack." He dropped back down to all fours and paced in front of the bedroom door while he waited. He was impatient, even as a pup, so I hurried through the rest of my sandwich. Once I was done, I picked Clay up and opened the bedroom door. The cats flew out of the doorway like bullets but then hissed when they realized I was holding the little food thief out of their reach.

"Stop it. Go to bed."

The cats gave one final hiss before they sauntered off to their beds. I didn't miss the glares they gave me before they both laid their heads on their paws. Assholes. I was surrounded by assholes, I thought as I took Clay into the bedroom and put him on the bed so I could strip down again. I changed into my wolf and hopped up onto the bed next to Clay. After I got comfortable, Clay rolled himself into a ball next to me, and we slept until late the next afternoon.

"COME ON. YOU have to get up." I shook Clay's shoulder hard enough to make his head loll to the side.

He opened one eye and frowned. "I don't want to." He tried to pull the sheet over his head, but I grabbed it and yanked it off his naked body.

"You have to. We have to work today or we'll get fired." I threw his work jeans at his head, followed by his T-shirt, underwear, and socks as he tried to bat each away. "Get up now, or I'll go get that pitcher of ice water out of the fridge and dump it over your head."

"Fuck off." He rolled onto his stomach and pulled the pillow over his head.

"Fine, you asked for it." I turned to leave but heard him move, so I stopped.

"Don't you fucking dare." He'd sat up and when I turned around he was stretching and then rubbing his eyes. "Why couldn't we just take the whole week off?"

"Because it's hard enough for both of us to get four days in a row off, let alone a week." It was true, and if it hadn't been for me needing to take care of Clay, I'd have gone to work during the full-moon phase. Thank God, Billy Ray was the one who approved time off. "Now get dressed. I made you a breakfast sandwich and there's coffee." I left him there, hoping this time I wouldn't come back to find him snoring. I was getting sick of being the one responsible for getting Clay out of bed in the mornings. Hell, I was getting sick of playing mommy in many ways, but I kept doing it because I still felt responsible for Clay's situation. Even though he'd bitten me, my conscience was still telling me it was my fault he'd lost his job.

It took him a few minutes, but he managed to get up and go into the bathroom, and when he emerged, he was fully dressed. He didn't say much as he gobbled down his breakfast and snatched up his travel mug on his way to the truck. Rolling my eyes, I followed, only stopping to lock the door before I climbed into the driver's seat.

We were halfway to the jobsite when Clay turned to me. "I'm sorry for being so hard to get out of bed. It took me two years to get used to getting up at seven every morning to work at the DMV. I had to set a dozen alarm clocks and put them a few steps from my bed and I still overslept a few times in those years. I suck at getting up. Even my mom gave up on waking me up nicely and started using a bullhorn."

I smiled when I thought about getting a bullhorn of my own or maybe one of those airhorns. I couldn't though, because I'd end up waking the rest of the RV park, and with my luck, Clay would still be the last one out of bed. I was happy with his apology. It was exactly what I needed from him that morning when I was feeling put upon and ready to give up. Clay certainly knew how to defuse what was sure to be a huge fight in the making.

We separated when we got to the site, and I was feeling pretty good after the full moon. Even with Clay's crankiness, I thought things were going well. But, of course, they couldn't always go well because then it wouldn't be my life.

"WHERE ARE THE fucking pizza rolls?" Clay slammed the freezer door shut and glared at me. He'd had a rough day at work before we were rained out early and sent home. Clay had been trying to pick a fight with me ever since we got in the truck for the drive home. So far, I'd resisted taking the bait, but it was getting mighty tempting to bitch right back.

"You ate the last of them a couple days ago. Maybe you can have hot pockets?" I planned on shopping in the morning. We were getting a rare Saturday off because of the rain, and I'd wanted to make the most out of the extra day without work by stocking up on supplies and doing a little cleaning around the RV so we could actually enjoy a Sunday without chores for once.

"I don't want hot pockets. I want pizza rolls." Clay threw himself on the couch and proceeded to sulk like a teenager.

"There's pizza-flavored ones in there. What's the difference?"

Glaring at me like I was an idiot, Clay grunted instead of responding.

"How about...you eat a couple of hot pockets and then we can fuck? You'll forget all about wanting pizza rolls after coming." I wasn't proud of what I was doing, but sex usually broke Clay out of whatever funk he was in and made him way more agreeable.

"I want pizza rolls."

"Then go buy some!" He'd found the end of my rope, and now I was spoiling for the fight to come.

"I don't want to get dressed to go out in the rain. You go get 'em."

"Fuck you. You're the one who wants them; you go."

Clay's eyes narrowed as he studied me. Maybe he was sizing me up to see if there was a weak spot he could exploit. Or maybe he was just trying to scare me into doing what he wanted—which had worked in the past—but not this time. I was going to stand my ground.

"Let's arm wrestle to see who goes."

"No, I'm not going." I opened the fridge to see what else was in there that might get his mind off the blasted pizza rolls.

"I'm not going either, but I want pizza rolls."

I shut the fridge door and turned on him. "So, you automatically think if we arm wrestle for it, you'll win and I'll have to go. I doubt your scrawny ass could beat me." I snorted and flexed my arm for him to see.

"I'll take my chances." He shrugged.

"Fine, I'll arm wrestle you but only if you agree to go get the pizza rolls and pick up the rest of the groceries for the week if I win. No deciding you'll eat hot pockets if you lose so you can stay home." I knew I had him. He hated grocery shopping, and there was no way he'd risk having to do it for pizza rolls.

Clay got off the couch and sauntered over to me. "I'll take those terms. But if I win, you'll get the pizza rolls and I get a blowjob when you get back." He sat on one of the stools by the small kitchen island and propped his arm on the table.

"Fine. It's not like you weren't going to get one anyway, but if you renege when I win, you're sleeping on the couch tonight." I sat down, too, and grasped his hand before bracing his elbow with my other.

"In your dreams, and I want ice cream bars for dessert since you're going out and all."

"Now, who's dreaming?"

"Are you ready?"

"Yep, go!"

I RAN FROM the truck to the store, and I was still soaking wet by the time I got inside. It was really pouring out. I cursed Clay again as I grabbed a cart and headed to the frozen food section. I was passing the deli counter when someone called my name, making me pause and turn and then startle when I saw my younger brother, Dante, standing there holding a box he'd just taken from the guy behind the counter.

"Dante, holy shit, you're all grown up." I don't know why I was so surprised that the teenager I'd left behind was now a man. He stepped in for an awkward hug before disengaging and punching me in the shoulder, hard.

"Fucker."

"What did I do now?" He couldn't be angry at me for leaving. He knew why I'd had to and had been one of the only people in the pack who'd supported my decision.

"You come back to town and you can't even come for a visit or, shit, maybe even give me a call?"

"I didn't think anyone would want to see me, except Mom and Dad, and you know why I'm avoiding that reunion."

"Yeah, I know, but you coulda called me. I miss you, and it sucks knowing you're back but don't want to see me." He kicked the wheel of my shopping cart and wouldn't make eye contact, as if he was ashamed of having admitted he missed me.

"I'm sorry. I missed you too. Hey, why don't I grab my groceries, and we can have a quick coffee or something at the snack bar? Catch up a little and I'll give you my number so you can call me whenever you want."

"Sounds good, but I don't have a whole lot of time. I'm meeting Hailey Ford at the theater to see the new X-Men movie." A grin split his face from ear to ear, and I laughed as I started pushing my cart to the back of the store where Clay's pizza rolls awaited me.

"You finally convinced her to go out with you, huh?" He'd been asking Hailey Ford out since they were in seventh grade, but she always shot him down.

"We've been dating for almost two years now. I think I'm going to ask her to marry me soon."

"No way! I can't believe my baby brother is old enough to get married." I stopped and grabbed three boxes of assorted pizza rolls and then made my way to the ice cream.

"Yeah, well, you've been gone a long time." He shrugged and snorted when I added two boxes of ice cream sandwiches to the cart. "Did you have a bunch of kids while you were away?"

"No, though a few toddlers would probably be easier to deal with than Clay."

"I heard you had yourself a boyfriend from up North."

I wheeled the cart to the self-checkout since I only had five items and started scanning. "I wouldn't exactly call him my boyfriend." I grabbed his deli box and scanned it before handing it back and running my debit card through the reader.

"I could have paid for my own supper, but thanks."

"I figured it would be quicker than waiting for you to figure out how to use the scanner." Dante had never been good with technology, but really, I'd just wanted to do something brotherly for him.

"I've gotten better with stuff. I was just a kid when you left, you know."

"Sixteen isn't exactly a helpless baby." I stuck my tongue out at him as I grabbed up my bags. "Even if Mom always treated you like you were still her little man."

"God, please, stop. She still calls me that in front of Hailey, and it's just as mortifying now as it was then." We got in line at the snack bar and ordered slushies instead of coffee, then found a booth. "Are you sure you have time right now? Your stuff is going to melt." He nodded to my frozen foods.

"Right now, I don't give a shit if I bring back slop for Clay to eat."

Dante raised an eyebrow. "Lover's spat?"

"More like my asshole of a roommate is an immature prick." I might have still been a little pissed about having to go out to get his fucking pizza rolls.

"Is that why you don't bring him home to the pack?"

"No, that's not why." I sucked on my straw for a good long while, trying to figure out if I could trust telling Dante about Clay, or if he'd run back and tell everyone that I had brought an infected into pack territory.

"Is it because Billy Ray is still hanging around?"

"No, though I'm surprised he didn't go back home after college."

"His family didn't want him, which is why he moved in with us." Dante's lips twisted into a snarl as my jaw dropped in surprise. "Oh, he didn't tell you that? I would have thought he'd have made sure it was the first thing out of his mouth, the little bastard."

"He lives with you and Mom and Dad?" It was almost inconceivable to me that Billy Ray would be living in my house with my family, who I'd had to leave because of him.

"Yep. In your room even."

"Why? I mean, why?"

"Because Mom and Dad thought you'd come to your senses, and they didn't want your bonded mate out on the street or to be honest, out trying to find someone else." Dante stared intently at me, watching for my reaction to what he was saying, but when he didn't get one, he asked again about Clay. "So why don't you bring Clay home and give them a reason to kick Billy Ray out?"

I sighed and let my head drop back so I could stare at the florescent lights hanging above us. "If I tell you something, you promise to keep it a secret?"

"I guess. I mean, yeah, sure. We're brothers. Keeping secrets from the 'rents is what we do, right?"

I lifted my head and looked him in the eyes. If I couldn't trust my only brother, who could I trust? "I need you to promise on Hailey's life that you won't breathe a word of what I'm about to tell you to anyone."

Dante's face turned serious and he nodded. "Okay, I swear on Hailey's life, but how bad can it be?"

I leaned forward so I could lower my voice. "Clay's infected. I infected him." It was his turn to stare slack-jawed at me. "I can't bring him anywhere near the pack, and now you know why." I sat back and waited for him to condemn me and tell me he was absolutely not going to keep a secret that big for me, blood ties or not.

"You infected him? You. The guy who always walked such a straight line that when you left I was sure that you had been brainwashed just like everyone was saying because you never broke any rule in your life. You broke the biggest rule of all for some human?"

"You thought I'd been brainwashed? Who would brainwash me and for what purpose?" The brainwashing story was news to me and the last thing I would have thought anyone would come up with to explain why I'd left.

"Don't change the subject. Tell me why you'd do it. Why would you infect someone?"

"He bit me."

Dante laughed so loud that the other people in the snack bar all gave us looks. "Now that's the funniest thing I ever heard."

I glared at him until he stopped sniggering. "It's true. And you want to know another secret? He's a fucking alpha."

"No, no way. Now I know you're lying because an infected can't be an alpha." Dante shook his head to emphasize his denial of what I was saying.

"It's true, and he's not the first infected I've met who's one. They lied to us all those years about what the infecteds are capable of, and their reasons for getting rid of them don't hold water after you know the truth." I hated having to burst my baby brother's bubble, but our pack's lies had gone on for too long.

Dante crossed his arms over his chest. "I don't believe you."

Fear struck me so hard it raised goosebumps on my arms. "You're going to tell the pack about Clay, aren't you?"

"No, fuck, Damian, I'm no snitch. Just because I think you're blowing smoke up my ass doesn't mean I'll rat you out to the pack." He raised one hand to scratch his chin. "If he's such a pain in your ass, why are you going through all this to protect him?"

Sighing, I shook my head. "I feel like he's my responsibility since it was my fault he got infected. On top of that, his beast calls to me, but it's more than those things too."

"Like what?"

"I can't explain it."

"Well he's got to be better than Billy Ray, right?" Dante grinned.

"He's really living in my room?" I still had a hard time believing it, and the more I thought about it, the angrier it made me that my parents were still choosing him over me.

"Yeah, sleeps in your bed and everything. You should have heard him the other night when he came home. He still thinks he has a chance with you." Dante looked at his phone. "Shit, I gotta get going."

I stood when he did, and he hugged me again, this time it was a lot less awkward. "Thanks for sitting with me for a bit."

"I'm glad I saw you. I really did miss you and hope we can get together while you're here. I also want to meet Clay."

"I'd like for you to meet him. Oh, that reminds me." I took out my phone and handed it to him. "Put your number in there, and I'll text you so you have mine."

He did so and handed it back. "I really gotta run or Hailey will kill me for being late."

"Okay, talk to you soon." He nodded, and I watched him walk away before I picked up my bags. I was sure the ice cream bars were a pile of mush, but after seeing my brother for the first time in five years, I didn't care if Clay threw a fit when I got home. It was his fault I was there in the first place. Asshole could deal with the consequences of cheating at arm wrestling.

Chapter Six

CLAY

Sitting at the counter, eating the pizza rolls I'd cheated to get, I watched Damian as he walked through the trailer, gathering dirty clothes. I knew better than to say anything. The way he was throwing shirts and socks into the basket told me he was in no mood for my bullshit. Something had to have happened while he was out. Though he was cranky when he left to go to the grocery store, he hadn't been uber pissed. I'd expected him to be in a better mood when he came home because that's how Damian worked. Give him some time to cool down by himself, and Damian usually went back to his easygoing self.

"I don't know why you can't put your socks in the fucking hamper. It's like living with a toddler who loses a sock and you find it under the couch cushions two months later." Damian stood from where he'd just fished one of my socks out from under the couch and aimed a pointed glare at me.

"It's the cats." He put a hand on his hip when I mumbled my excuse, making me feel defensive. "It's true. You know how they are, and I swear they do that shit to make me look bad because they're assholes."

"You'd blame anything to get out of taking responsibility for your own shit." Damian grabbed the full basket and carried it to the bedroom, where I was sure he'd find even more of my dirty laundry to bitch about. "I wish you'd grow up a little." He threw that last bit back at me over his shoulder.

Instead of arguing, I finished my meal and then got up and washed the plate and glass I'd used. I realized I took advantage of Damian's guilt. He did most of the housework and all the grocery shopping. I should try to pitch in more. I silently vowed to do just that, but then Damian howled in pain from the bedroom, and I forgot what I was thinking about as I rushed to see what had happened.

Damian was hopping around on one foot, hissing and groaning as he rubbed the toes on the other. As I watched, he plopped down on the bed and pulled the injured body part up to look at it. "I stubbed my fucking pinkie toe on the end of the fucking bed." He didn't look at me as he told me what he'd done, which was good because I was stifling a snicker.

"I thought you'd lost an arm or something with the way you screamed." I managed not to laugh even as I picked on him just a little.

"It fucking hurts. What, you've never stubbed a toe before?" He sat there rubbing his toe and still hissing occasionally at the pain.

"No, I've stubbed my toe plenty of times, just don't remember shrieking like a chick when I did." I knew the minute the words were out of my mouth that I shouldn't have said them. I could smell his anger as it permeated the air around him. I really needed to stop poking at him if I wanted him to get over the pissy mood he'd been in since he came home. "I'm sorry. I was just joking." My eyes strayed to the laundry basket that was overflowing now that he'd picked up everything in the bedroom. "How about I go throw a couple of loads in the washer so you don't have to walk on your hurt foot?"

He jerked around to look at me. "Are you being serious right now?"

"Totally. I mean, it's probably my turn to do it anyway, and if you stubbed that toe bad enough, putting on shoes will hurt. I'll just take the truck up to the lodge and put the clothes in. It's no big deal." I shrugged as I bent to grab the basket. When I stood and settled it on my hip, I couldn't miss the expression on his face. I almost rolled my eyes at the soft look he was giving me, but I refrained from doing it because I figured it would only send him back into his dark mood.

"Thank you." Damian smiled as he lay back on the bed and stared at the ceiling. "There are quarters on the dresser, and the laundry soap is in the closet by the door."

"I know where the soap is." Sometimes I thought Damian thought I was an idiot. "I'll be back in a few." I went out and grabbed the enormous bottle of laundry soap and the keys before slipping on my shoes and running through the rain to the truck. The basket went on the seat next to me as I started the engine and then drove to the lodge.

When I was leaning over to grab the basket, a noise caught my attention. It was the familiar buzzing of Damian's phone when he received a text message. I usually wasn't nosy, but the phone was right there and the name of the texter caught my eye.

Hot Grocery Store Guy: Hey!

Who the fuck was hot grocery story guy, and why was he texting Damian? I got my answer when the preview of the next text popped up on the screen.

Oh, hell no. I restarted the engine and turned the truck around to head back to the trailer. Fuck the laundry, I was getting an explanation for this right fucking now. I slammed the pickup door so hard I was surprised the window didn't shatter. Just the thought of Damian stepping out on me with some random dude he met at the store had me seeing red. I reached around and scratched the back of my head, like that would calm my beast, which was egging me on.

I threw the door open with so much force that it bounced off the wall and came back to hit me, but I didn't let that stop me from charging in to find Damian by the kitchen counter. He was swaying to the music he had playing as he prepared some meat that was probably going to be our supper. His shocked look would have been comical if I hadn't been so pissed off at him.

"You're back. Did you forget the soap?" He started for the closet, but I held up his phone and he stopped. "Oh, I forgot it in the pickup again, huh?" He reached for it, but I jerked it away before he could grab it. "What the fuck is up with you?"

"Want to tell me who hot grocery store guy is? Or did you assume you could just fuck around behind my back, and I'd never find out about it?"

He looked confused for a moment and then it looked like something dawned on him and he laughed, which made me even madder. "It's my brother. Give me my phone and let me see what he wants." He held out his hand, but I wasn't ready to believe him just yet.

"What do you mean it's your brother? Are you some sort of pervert?"

"What? No, it's just his sense of humor. I met him at the store and gave him my phone to put his number in and that's what he saved it under. He thinks he's funny. Now give it over so I can see what he wanted."

I studied him to see if I could tell if he was lying. I couldn't tell, but the whole story sounded pretty fishy to me. "I thought you were avoiding your family."

"My parents, yeah, and it's not like I planned on seeing Dante; he was just there. I wasn't going to ignore my little brother. Give me my phone."

"Why didn't you tell me you ran into your brother?" I was still suspicious, but I handed over his phone.

"I was still a little pissed when I got back, in case you didn't notice."

"I noticed that you seemed even more pissed than when you left. Was that because of your brother?"

"Yeah, well, no, it was because he told me Billy Ray is living at my house, sleeping in my fucking bed. How do you like that shit?" He looked down at his phone, checked his messages and grinned, but then when he looked back at me, it dropped off his face. "And what happened to you not giving a shit about if I went out and fucked someone else? We're not exclusive, remember?"

My beast practically punched me in the back of my brain, but I gritted my teeth as I fought what it wanted. "That's right. We're not some fucking couple who's all lovey dovey and pledging our undying love to one another. It was my wolf that got pissy. Sometimes I can't control the emotions it makes me feel, so don't get all excited that I was jealous or something because I'm not."

"Oh, really, you weren't jealous at all when you thought this message was from some hot guy I'd met at the grocery store?" He obviously didn't believe that it was just my beast making me crazy. His smirk pissed me off even more than him thinking I'd be jealous over the thought of him with someone else.

"No, I wasn't. I don't give a shit if you fuck every guy from here to...whatever fucking state is next to this shit hole." I'd stepped in closer, but it seemed that my attempt to intimidate him this time wasn't working because he stood up taller so the inch he had on me was apparent. "You could go fuck Billy Ray, for all I care." It was the one thing I was most afraid of happening. I knew if he did, I'd lose him forever, so it made my point that much finer.

"Really? Well, maybe I will then." He spat the words at me as he turned around and stomped off toward the bedroom.

"You go ahead and do that. I'll be at the bar finding my own piece of ass." I grabbed my sweatshirt, because although it wasn't cold out, it was still pouring. Since I didn't have a car, I'd have to hoof it and hope I could hitch a ride to town.

"That's fine. Go fuck as many guys as you want, but don't be surprised if I'm not here when you get back."

"It's fine. I'm sure your parents will want you to stay for breakfast when you're done fucking their houseguest anyway." I couldn't stop myself from poking at the fact that Billy Ray was living with his parents and had to duck when he threw a boot at me. Almost running, I made it to the door just as the other boot hit the wall next to it. He was bitching as I slammed the door behind me.

It was a good thing I'd put on my pants before I'd headed to the lodge to do laundry or I wouldn't have had my wallet with me. I pulled my hood up over my head and walked down the lane to the entrance of the park. An engine alerted me to someone slowly inching up behind me. At first I thought it was Damian coming to apologize for being a dick, and I already had my quick and biting response at the ready, but it turned out to be the guy from a few spots down who appeared to live there year-round.

"Hey, you need a lift?" he asked out the window as he pulled up next to me.

"Yeah, you going into town?" He nodded and popped the locks so I could get in. "You know any good dive bars?"

"Sure, depends on what you're looking for." He side-eyed me and I figured he'd seen enough of me and Damian around to have gotten the idea that our relationship wasn't just a platonic friendship.

"I'd like to get my dick sucked." I tried being blunt, which made him bark out a laugh. "By a dude."

"I know just the place." He gave me a nod and didn't ask any more questions as he drove. Soon we were in town, and he pulled up outside a small bar. "This should do ya."

"Thanks for the ride." I popped the door open and jumped out into the rain, shutting it on his response of no problem. The bar was either not very popular or the weather was keeping people at home, but I didn't care. I wasn't actually looking for anyone to screw, no matter what I'd told Damian or the neighbor. I was just looking for a drink.

Chapter Seven

BILLY RAY

The lights in the club were pulsing along with the thumping music as I sat at the bar nursing my third drink of the night. The pickings were slim for a Saturday—must have been the rain keeping people home. I was thinking about leaving, but then the air around me changed in a way that had my beast sitting at attention and me swiveling my head around to find the reason for the sudden change in atmosphere. And there it—or should I say he—was.

Clay walked through the club like he was a man with a mission, and when his eyes landed on me, I felt like he'd found the objective. One side of his mouth drew up in a smirk as he made his way to me and settled on the stool to my left. "Well, well, well, Mr. Boss Man's out on the town tonight, huh?" He raised a hand to get the bartender's attention and ordered a beer.

"Even the boss needs to unwind sometimes." Looking around for Damian, I expected him to join us at any moment, since it seemed the two of them were always joined at the hip.

"He's not coming." Clay paid for his beer and gulped down half before turning on his stool to face me. I tried not to look disappointed, but his grunt told me I'd failed. "Sorry, you'll have to make do with me."

What did he mean, I'd have to make do with him? "I was actually just about to leave." I downed the rest of my drink, making myself cringe, and then made to get up, but he grabbed my arm.

"Sit with me, Billy Ray. I've had a shit night, and since you're part of the reason for that, you could at least keep me company while I drink myself into a stupor."

Settling back onto my stool, I pulled my arm from his grasp. "I'm part of the reason you're having a bad night?"

"Yep." He chugged his beer and motioned to order another. He pointed to my empty glass, too, but didn't say anything to expound on how I was responsible for his troubles.

"Care to tell me how I figure into your woes?"

He side-eyed me and then snorted. "Who the hell talks like that?"

"Like what?"

"Woes? Who says woes?"

"I do, I guess, but if you don't understand the meaning of the word, I can rephrase the question using simpler terms."

Clay turned to face me and our eyes met. I realized I was playing with fire when it came to baiting him. "I'm not stupid, and if you think you can use your superior intellect to intimidate me, you have another think coming." He punctuated his sentence with a low rumbling growl, and my answering whine was automatic and made him grin.

"You're not supposed to use that on someone when you're in their territory. It's a major breach of pack protocol when you're visiting." I hated the way I responded to Clay. Having fought off the advances of alpha males all my life, I'd never had one who affected me the way he did. I didn't like it.

"I didn't do it intentionally. I don't really know how to control this thing that lives inside me." Clay nodded to the bartender when he dropped off our drinks and once again guzzled his beer.

"That's to be expected if you're newly infected, but you might want to be more careful. If you challenge someone from the pack like that, they're not liable to cut you slack for being new to this." I picked up my drink and sipped it.

"I know. Damian told me how you guys down here handle my kind." He flicked his beer bottle a couple of times with a finger. "Pretty shitty of you all, if you ask me."

"I can't argue that it's not." I didn't know what Clay wanted from me, but he seemed like he needed someone to listen to him vent, so I decided to be that person. "Why don't we go sit in one of the booths? We can talk without being overheard."

Clay stared at me for a moment before grabbing his beer and standing. He waited for me to gather my drink, then followed me to the back corner where there was an empty table. After sitting, I'd assumed he'd take a seat across from me, but he followed me onto the bench, making me have to scoot over to the wall.

Once seated, Clay stared at me for a moment. "Something's different about you tonight. You smell"—he leaned in and sniffed the air around me—"off."

Shrugging, I tried not to look uncomfortable about him invading my personal space or about him telling me I smelled funny. "Probably just my cologne," I lied, not wanting to discuss my hormonal changes with someone who was practically a stranger.

Clay seemed to get the hint and sat back before he changed the subject. "Why do you live with Damian's family?"

The question took me by surprise, but now I had an idea of how I was to blame for his shitty night. "Who told him?"

"He ran into his brother at the store."

"Ah, of course, that would have been one of the first things Dante would tell him. He never liked me and blamed me when Damian left." It hadn't been my fault. Damian made his own choices. Even after I'd offered to transfer to another college, he'd told me he was going to leave whether I stayed or not.

"Can you blame him?"

"You don't know the whole story."

"Then tell me the whole story. I'm sick of having to guess why I just got kicked out of the RV."

"He kicked you out?" That was not at all what I'd expected had happened. Clay always seemed like the hothead of the two, and I'd figured he'd probably stormed out, leaving Damian to worry about where he'd gone.

"Yeah, he kicked me out. Told me to go find someone else to fuck." Clay growled again before draining his beer and immediately signaling the waitress for another. "Fucker promised me a blowjob if I won at arm wrestling too."

"Wow."

"No, not wow. It's fucked up. He knows I got nowhere to go, and that camper is too damn small, for the time being, for two people who hate each other." He looked around the bar as he talked. I had a feeling I wasn't getting the whole story, but I let it slide because, of course, I'd only get one side, and it would be skewed to make Clay look like the injured party.

He did look upset, though, which made me do something not so smart, but doing the occasional stupid thing was something I was known for. "I have a hotel room. There's two beds. You're welcome to take one of them for the night."

His brow furrowed as he stared at me. "Why do you have a hotel room? Did you get thrown out too?"

"No, nothing that dramatic. I just need my own space sometimes. Usually the weekend after the full moon, if you get what I'm saying." Hoping I didn't need to spell it out for him, I lifted my drink to my lips, but his bray of laughter made me spill some of it down the front of my shirt. I grabbed a napkin and dabbed at the wetness while I waited for him to calm down. It took longer than I thought necessary.

"Let me get this straight. You rent a motel room for a weekend because you're not allowed to have boys in your room?" He chortled again but held up his hand when I opened my mouth to rebut him. "No wonder Damian left if his mommy and daddy were that strict."

Rolling my eyes, I considered leaving, but then I remembered I'd just offered him a bed. "It's not that I can't take people back to the Maccon's house, but I choose not to. It's a respect thing."

Clay nodded. "I get that, I guess. So you'd really let me crash in your room?"

"Why not?" I could think of a thousand reasons why not, and one of them was the way Clay was eyeing me like I was the biggest, juiciest steak he'd ever seen, but it would be impolite to rescind the offer.

"Okay, well then, let's get shitfaced." Clay raised his beer bottle and waited until I clinked my almost empty glass against the neck of it.

"You're going to need something stronger than beer if you're going to get drunk." We had a high metabolism, only strong liquor drunk quickly would do the job, but I was sure he knew that too.

"I know. This place have a liquor store?"

I shook my head. "No, but I know the guy behind the bar. I can get him to sell me a bottle under the counter. What do you want?"

"Vodka, and get a big bottle." Clay pulled his wallet out and insisted on shoving a fifty in my hand when I tried to wave him off. "You're paying for the room so it's only fair I pay for the drinks." Once again, I was having second thoughts about my offer. When he put it that way, it sounded like a hookup, and that wasn't what I'd been thinking when I'd offered. He scooted out of the booth and stood while I got up. "I'll meet you outside." He left after I nodded.

Randy was behind the bar and had no problem selling me a bottle of vodka—with a hefty surcharge—making the handoff when he gave me the umbrella I'd asked him to stash for me earlier. I thanked him and went out into the rain to find Clay. He was standing under the overhang from the building and waited for me to open my umbrella so we could both benefit from its coverage.

"Did you get the bottle?"

I held it up to show him and he grinned. "Did you drive, or did Damian drop you off?"

"I hitched a ride with a guy from the RV park." He looked around the lot. "Where's your Jeep?"

"It's at the motel, but we can walk. It's just over that way." I pointed to the lighted sign of the Royal Inn. Unfortunately, the neon A and L had gone out and now it was just the Roy Inn.

"Looks classy." Clay took the umbrella from me, since he was taller, and we walked in step through the bar's parking lot to the hotel. I used my body to direct him to the stairs. Once on the second level and under the roof, Clay closed the umbrella and followed me to my room at the far end of the row of doors and waited while I used the key card to let us in.

"It's not great, but at least it's clean. The owner doesn't rent by the hour so that keeps the junkies out." I bent down and took off my wet boots as he toed off his sneakers and walked past to look at the room.

"It's not as bad as I thought it would be." He flopped down on the bed. "This place got glasses or are we drinking out of the bottle?"

"I think there's a couple of plastic ones in the bathroom." I went into the tiny bathroom, and sure enough, there were a couple of plastic cups wrapped in cellophane on the sink. I held them up to show Clay. He grunted as he unscrewed the cap off the bottle of vodka and patted the bed for me to sit by him.

Unwrapping the glasses as I went, I then held one out for him to fill as I sat. He poured and set the bottle on the ground before turning to look at me. That's when I realized it was the first time he was seeing my face with enough light to see that I was wearing makeup. I threw back the contents of my glass and waited for what I knew was coming.

"Are you wearing makeup?"

"Can I have more?" Holding out my glass, I swallowed back the defiant words wanting to escape in defense of my choice to wear makeup.

He poured me a double shot and added as much to his cup too. "I didn't mean to upset you. I was just surprised; that's all." He shrugged.

So, Damian hadn't told Clay what being an omega meant. Interesting, or annoying depending on how you looked at it. I was going with annoying since it now fell to me to explain my particular lot in life to Clay. "Hasn't Damian taught you about packs and the different members within them?"

He shook his head and drank before answering me. "He tries to tell me shit, but I'm not really interested."

"You really should get interested. If you were born into a pack, you wouldn't need to learn all this stuff because you'd have picked up on all of it just growing up around it. You'd know your place in the pack along with everyone else's."

"What's the deal with the mate bond?" He poured more into his glass and then scooted up the bed so he could sit with his back against the pillows and headboard, legs splayed out in front of him. I stood and walked around the bed, thinking I'd go sit on the other one, but he grabbed my arm, stopping me. "Sit here with me." When I hesitated, he added, "It will be easier for me to pour your drinks for you."

"Sure, that's why." I didn't believe he didn't have ulterior motives for wanting me to sit on the bed. The man oozed pheromones, and I completely understood how Damian had ended up with him.

"I'm not going to rape you, if that's what you're worried about."

Rolling my eyes, I crawled over him and sat on the bed in much the same position he was in. "That's not what I was worried about."

"It's not like you're not cute and all, but I prefer my men willing." Clay winked and once again drained his glass. He appeared to be serious about getting drunk. "So, you were just about to tell me about the mate bond thing, and what the hell happened with you and Damian that made him run as fast and as far as he could to get away from it."

"I never said I was going to tell you any of that." I couldn't tell Clay about Damian and me, but I could tell him about the bond in general. "The bond is exactly what it says it is. There are pairs of bonded mates, usually indicated by the bicolored irises, which you probably already know."

"Yeah, I know all that. Damian told me, but what does it mean? I mean, if you can choose not to be with the person who's supposedly meant for you, then why have it at all?" Clay looked confused, which only made him look more attractive.

I raised my glass, but as that thought went through my mind, I decided to slow down with the booze. Nothing good could come from me and Clay hooking up, which was a distinct possibility if our inhibitions were lowered and our beastly instincts were allowed to take over. Since he wasn't slowing down, it was up to me to be the responsible one.

I needed to decide how much I was going to tell him. I'd been doing some research on infecteds and mate bonds. I knew some things, but how much I should reveal to Clay—who knew almost nothing about how packs worked—I wasn't sure. I decided to give him the basics and withhold the things I thought I should talk over with Damian first.

"No one knows why it's there, but I've heard it's one way our ancestors guide us. Usually those pairs with the mate bond end up becoming the leaders, or a force for some sort of change within the packs. Packs who have members with the mate bond sometimes spend millions of dollars and years trying to find the mate for that person."

"No shit?"

"No shit. My pack sent out feelers the day I was born."

"So, your pack must have sucked if they couldn't find the guy in the next state." Clay snorted and drained his glass again.

"No, they didn't suck. Damian's pack leaders were hiding that they had a member who had the sign. The alpha and his family were afraid that if Damian found his mate, he'd take over the pack, and they'd lose their position just like the Maccons lost theirs to the Luptons five generations ago."

"Oh, a little pack intrigue going on, is there?"

I nodded before giving him a little history lesson. "The Maccons are pretty vocal about their views of the Luptons. They've been rivals forever. They started out in two separate packs, but as the area started getting more populated, they found there wasn't room for two packs. They made a treaty and joined together. The Maccon's alpha ended up being the stronger of the two and therefore was put in the leadership position. Three generations later the Luptons had a daughter born with the mate bond. She got married to someone in the pack, because back then finding your mate was a hell of a lot harder, and most people just went on with their lives like it wasn't there. But then one day her bonded mate came through town and that was it for the first husband. The mate turned out to be an extremely powerful alpha, and that was the end of the Maccon's reign. Been bad blood between them ever since."

"Huh, wonder why Damian never told me any of this shit." Clay looked into his empty glass, and a frown creased his brow. "Damn, empty again." He filled his glass and offered me a refill, but I still hadn't drunk what he'd poured earlier. "If you don't hurry up, I'm going to end up drinking this whole bottle on my own."

"It's fine. I don't care much for straight vodka. And Damian has always kept to himself, which is probably why he didn't tell you about his family, or why he wanted to leave so badly."

His eyes narrowed as he looked at me. "I thought he left because of you."

"He did in a way, I guess. But it had more to do with his family wanting to get back into power and thinking he was the way to do it because of who I am and what's possible if we mated."

"So, he'd be more powerful if you guys,"—Clay made a crude gesture with his hands indicating sex—"and he'd be the alpha of the pack?"

"It's not just that." I shook my head because I was still shocked over how little Clay knew about everything related to lycanthropy and pack structure.

"Okay, so tell me what else there is."

Standing, I put my drink on the nightstand and pulled my shirt up over my head. I didn't look at him as I unbuttoned my pants, afraid of what I'd see on his face when he got a look at what I was wearing under my normal street clothes. I'd never been ashamed of who I was, but seeing the judgment on other men's faces when I revealed my *secret* still hurt. Once I stood in front of Clay in only the matching satin camisole and panties, I raised my eyes to meet his.

Chapter Eight

CLAY

Staring up at Billy Ray, who was standing there in women's underwear, I wondered what him being a cross-dresser had to do with anything. I opened my mouth to ask what his preference for silk had to do with anything, but he held up his hand to stop me as if he already knew what I was going to say and didn't want to hear it.

"You're a werewolf. Use your other senses for a minute, and tell me if you can figure out what's different about me." When I just sat there unblinking, he rolled his eyes and put his hand on his hip. "Just reach back and touch your beast for a minute, and then let it tell you what it can detect that you're missing."

It was my turn to roll my eyes, but I did as he instructed and thought about the beast living inside me. A low rumble shook my chest as if just thinking about the beast made it want to make its presence known. As soon as I let it in a little, my sense of smell grew more acute. Since contracting lycanthropy, all my senses were enhanced, but never as much as when the beast was in control. The alcohol helped me get in touch with it.

Billy Ray smiled as his beast's own guttural sound greeted mine. "Good, now just let it tell you what it already knows."

It's hard to explain how it feels when there are two distinctly separate minds in your head, but Billy Ray was right. My wolf knew right away that something was off about Billy Ray, and it was something more than just his scent that made me think of the meadow full of flowers in summer that I'd noticed earlier. When the realization hit me, I didn't believe it. How could it be? "You're female?" He nodded, looking pleased as he sat on the edge of the bed. "But how? I mean, you're a dude."

"I'm bigendered which means there are times when my gender identity matches that of my genitalia, but just as often, it doesn't."

"I have no idea what that means..." What the fuck? My mind was reeling, partially due to the fact that my beast was still close, but also because all of a sudden Billy Ray looked much more attractive to it.

"One body, two genders. It means that I can be either male or female. Take today for example, I felt more feminine than masculine, and one of the ways for me to express that is by choosing clothing that fits how I feel."

"So, do you want to be a woman?" Still not able to wrap my mind around it, I asked a stupid question that I wished I could take back when Billy Ray looked like he wanted to punch me.

"I'm not going to physically change my body. What good would that do me when I'm just as likely to wake up feeling like my male parts fit just right? I make do with what I have when I'm feeling like my body doesn't match. Thankfully, it's not as bad for me as it is for some people."

"I'm sorry. I don't know anything about being genderbending, or whatever it is you called it." Again, he looked upset, and I knew I'd gotten the word wrong, but it was the first one that came to mind. I tried to think of anything I'd heard about different gender identities, and the only thing my mind could dredge up was something I'd read on Twitter. "So what are your pronouns?"

Billy Ray laughed, but then surprised me by throwing his arms around my neck and hugging me. That turned out to be a really bad idea on his part because my beast liked the way he felt pressed against me. If I was being totally honest, the human part of me didn't much mind it either. I wrapped my arms around him and held him tight until he tried to pull back so he could look me in the eyes, and once again the similarity to Damian's struck me mute.

"I'm okay with he and him most of the time because I don't broadcast when I feel more feminine except when I'm in private or with people I trust. But if you get to know the cues, I appreciate it when people make the effort to use the ones that fit me at that time."

Immediately, my mind switched gears, and Billy Ray became she because my beast recognized Billy Ray as female. Maybe the pronoun thing wouldn't be too hard after all. Billy Ray shifted just a bit, and her mouth formed a perfect O of surprise when she felt what pressing her body next to mine had done to me.

"This is a really bad idea."

I nodded in agreement, but that didn't stop me from leaning in and brushing my lips across hers. A little sigh escaped Billy Ray's lips as she opened for me, and I took advantage of it to slip my tongue into her mouth. The kiss lasted only a few seconds, but it was long enough for my beast to start chanting for me to lay claim to Billy Ray, causing me to disengage. Was it me who was attracted to the person in my lap, or was my beast the one pushing me in that direction? I hated feeling unsure because I felt like it was the biggest underlying problem I had with my relationship with Damian.

"Maybe we should just go to sleep." Billy Ray pushed herself away from my chest, and I let her go. The tent in the front of her panties drew my eyes downward, and when she noticed, she quickly grabbed a pillow and put it in front of her to cover her arousal.

"Sleep with me." The words just popped out. I didn't mean to say them, and I could see by the look on Billy Ray's face that she thought I meant fuck, not sleep, so I jumped to clear up the misunderstanding. "I didn't mean sex. I just thought, maybe, you could sleep in the bed with me. I've sort of gotten used to having someone there next to me." I wasn't going to get into the dreams I had of hunting and killing, and how Damian's presence usually kept me from freaking out when I woke up craving bloody, raw meat. I didn't know Billy Ray well enough to confide my deepest darkests. Hell, I hadn't even told Damian the reason I woke up shaking and sweating some nights.

She shook her head. "I really feel like that would be a mistake. I need to use the restroom." She clambered off the bed and went into the bathroom before I could say anything more.

After picking up the half-full bottle of vodka, I didn't bother with using the cup, instead gulping it from the bottle while considering the things Billy Ray had told me. I now knew more of why Damian had left his pack behind, and why there was so much hostility against his family. Knowing Damian as well as I did, I knew being used as a pawn in their quest for power had to have pissed him off. And then there was Billy Ray. What could I say about that? It was too weird for me to digest in such a short time, and I still had lots of questions.

"Do you want the lights on or off?" Billy Ray stood by the light switch while she waited for my reply. She'd washed the makeup off her face but was still wearing the silky undergarments that, to me, only made her masculinity more pronounced. I'd never have thought I'd be one who'd get turned on by a guy in women's underwear, but damn, I had to adjust myself to take the pressure off my cock. "Well?"

"Huh?" I forgot the question.

"Lights. On or off?" I couldn't be sure, but I think Billy Ray might have been trying to suppress a smile as she stood there staring at me.

"Off is good, but I'm going to turn on this lamp until I've finished this bottle." Reaching over, I flicked on the lamp that sat on the nightstand between the beds as she flipped off the overhead and then walked over. Just when I thought she'd climb into bed with me, she turned and pulled back the bedspread on the other bed. I guzzled down the vodka and let the burn settle in my stomach.

"Good night, Clay." She settled on her side, facing me, under just the sheet and closed her eyes.

"Good night, don't let the bed bugs bite."

"You forgot the sleep tight bit." She didn't open her eyes but finally allowed herself to smile.

I put the empty bottle on the floor and stood to peel off my clothes—not failing to notice that Billy Ray had opened her eyes to watch—before flopping back onto the bed in just my boxer briefs. "Fuck that, I'm serious about the bed bugs. Who knows what sort of shit this place has crawling all over the mattresses."

"I'm sure you'll survive. Go to sleep." Billy Ray rolled over and sighed.

"Fine." I turned off the lamp and tried to get comfortable on the unfamiliar bed. Good thing I was drunk because otherwise there was no way I'd have been able to fall asleep on that rock-hard pillow.

"STOP IT, CLAY."

I heard the muttered words, but I couldn't do as they asked. Waking up with a steel-hard cock pressed between the softest satiny skin, I had no way to stop my hips from moving to get a little friction. I didn't know what Damian was complaining about. He usually didn't mind when I woke him up on our day off for a morning quickie before dozing off again, only to wake up hours later to eat a leisurely breakfast. A hand reached back and grasped my hair when I bent my head to nuzzle his neck.

"Goddamn it, Clay. I said stop it." He yanked my hair hard enough to kill the mood, and I opened my eyes to find, not Damian in my arms, but Billy Ray. The night before came crashing back to me as I released him and jumped out of bed.

"Fuck! What the fuck, Billy Ray?"

"Don't what the fuck me, mister." Billy Ray sat up in the bed and glared at me. I opened my mouth but then closed it when I realized I'd been in the wrong bed, not the other way around, and I couldn't remember how I'd gotten there. "Yeah, you're the one who crawled into my bed and then refused to leave. And FYI, using your beast's powers over a weaker wolf to get your way in a situation like that is really shitty." She or maybe she was a he again—damn this was so confusing and it was too early for me to care to try to figure out—crossed her arms over her chest.

"Are you always this bitchy in the morning?" Smooth, real smooth.

"Are you trying to imply that because I'm feminine, I'm bitchy?" She, yep, Billy Ray was full-on she and narrowed her eyes at me as if she expected me to try to talk my way out of the trouble I'd apparently just gotten myself into.

"No. Guys can be bitchy too." I shrugged and absentmindedly scratched my balls before it dawned on me that it wasn't polite to scratch your privates in front of a woman.

"Well, I have good reason to be upset with you right now." She got out of the bed and picked up her jeans.

"I'm sorry. I don't even remember how I ended up in your bed."

Billy Ray cocked her head at me and narrowed her eyes before nodding. "I guess I can believe that. You were pretty drunk." She shoved her legs in her pants and then went to a small travel bag and pulled out a clean shirt. "I think maybe you should go home and talk to Damian."

I snorted. "Yeah and have him tell me to get the hell out again? No thanks."

She sighed, and after pulling the shirt on over her head, she pointed at me. "You need to be a better listener."

"Huh?" How was Damian kicking me out my fault for not listening?

"You said he was angry and didn't want to give you a blowjob he was supposed to give you. Did he actually tell you to leave?" She waited while I thought about it, but I'm sure she saw when I realized Damian hadn't actually kicked me out. In truth, I'd twisted it in my head to make it feel like he had when he hadn't stopped me from leaving. "Yeah, that's what I thought. He was venting and being a man; you took it personally and did probably the worst thing you could, which was to walk out and leave him simmering."

"Does this sort of wisdom come from being feminine?" I ducked to avoid the pillow Billy Ray threw at my head.

"No, you idiot. This sort of wisdom comes from not being a Neanderthal. Now get dressed and go home." Billy Ray threw my clothes at me. "Tell him you're sorry for being a jerk and listen to him this time instead of getting pissy that he's angry at something that has nothing to do with you at all."

I RAN BILLY Ray's advice through my mind during the ride back to the RV Park in the back of a taxi. Still unsure of how to get Damian to forgive me for picking a fight, telling him I didn't care if he fucked someone else, and then leaving him when he obviously needed someone, I got out of the car and walked slowly to the door of the camper. It was unlocked, meaning Damian was awake and probably waiting for me to come home so he could tear me a new one. I stepped in, and Stumple and Grumpkin both greeted me at the door, but I ignored them to look around for Damian. He wasn't in the living area or kitchen.

"Damian?" I called out to let him know I was home, but there was no answer from the back part of the trailer. I knew he wouldn't leave the door unlocked if he was going anywhere, plus the truck was parked outside, so he couldn't have gone far. He had to be there. I was getting a little peeved at him. I knew he was mad, but if he thought ignoring me was the way to get that across, he was wrong. "Damian?" I asked as I opened the bedroom door to find the room empty. Where the hell was he?

I walked out and asked the cats where their owner was, but if they knew, they weren't telling. I stood in the middle of the living room, trying to think of where he'd go, when the door opened and Damian stepped in, carrying a basket of folded laundry under his arm. He didn't even glance in my direction, instead taking the clothes back to the bedroom, so I followed.

"I wondered where you were. I was worried for a minute when you weren't here and the door was unlocked." I stood in the narrow doorway and leaned against the jamb.

"It's not like the world stops turning because you decide to run out on it." Damian took a stack of underwear out of the basket and went about separating mine from his before putting them in their respective drawers.

"I wanted to tell you I'm sorry for leaving like I did." I stepped into the room and closed the distance between us. He stopped what he was doing, and I heard him sniff to scent the air.

He shot up and stood toe-to-toe with me to get in my face. "You were with Billy Ray last night?"

"I ran into him at the bar, but—"

"You spent the night with Billy fucking Ray!" He shouted the words into my face. Spittle flew from his lips to land on my skin before he leaned in and sniffed me as if he needed to make sure.

"Nothi—"

"Shut up! Just shut the hell up for once, Clay!" He turned away from me, and I could see he was trying to calm himself, but he practically bounced with angry energy.

My beast growled when it picked up on Damian's agitation. Damian whirled around. Instead of the deference he usually showed when my beast made itself known, he glowered at me, and a rumble of his own made me jump back. He was challenging me. I don't know how I knew it, but I did, and I also knew it was because of Billy Ray. I wasn't sure what came next. Did we fight? I didn't want to fight Damian over Billy Ray because my human mind wasn't even that interested in him, but my beast had other ideas and it propelled my body forward.

Damian didn't back down as I crowded him. He lifted his chin and stared defiantly at me. "I know you're stronger than me, but that doesn't mean I have to let you take what's mine without a fight."

His words hit me hard in the gut because I realized no matter how much Damian claimed he didn't want the mate bond or the man who came with it, he would always be linked to Billy Ray. I'd never have that with him, or anyone for that matter. I stepped back and hung my head. "You're right. Billy Ray belongs to you and you to him. I'm just getting in the way of what's meant to be."

"Fuck you. You don't get to be the injured party here. I've done nothing but make sure you're taken care of, and I even tried to love you, but you're just a stubborn prick. I just can't believe you took the first chance you could and fucked Billy Ray, probably knowing it was the one thing that I couldn't get over."

I opened my mouth to tell him I hadn't fucked anyone, but he sucker-punched me in the stomach before stomping out. Hunched over, holding my stomach, I listened as he got in the truck and peeled out on the gravel road. I knew what I had to do, but I wasn't looking forward to it. After taking a few minutes to let the pain ebb, I grabbed a duffel from the closet and started throwing clothes into it. I wasn't sure where I was going, but I knew I needed to get gone before Damian came back or there'd be trouble.

Chapter Nine

DAMIAN

Rage. A red haze colored my vision, but as soon as I was on the highway heading into town, it lifted. Fuck. I'd punched Clay. Part of me wanted to turn around. Go back and tell him I was sorry and listen to what he had to say, but the other part of me—the part that was seething with fury at the images my brain kept conjuring up of Clay's body entwined with Billy Ray's—knew going back was a bad idea. My beast was too close to the surface, and it was pissed that Clay had taken something from him. Even though at the same time, he realized that we belonged to Clay.

Pulling over to the shoulder, I sat for a minute before taking my phone out and sending a text to Dante. It only took a few minutes for him to text me back, and with my destination known, I merged back into traffic. I was probably about to do something monumentally stupid, but I couldn't stop myself. The need to lash out at both Clay and Billy Ray was too strong, and I knew just the way to get my revenge.

One sharp rap on the flimsy door brought footsteps from within. The door jerked open, and I could only assume that Billy Ray had looked out the peephole before he'd answered because the look he was giving me was most accurately described as pissed-off deer in the headlights.

"Billy Ray." Nodding my head, I stepped quickly past her into the room. Her scent, wildflowers in summer, would drive my beast wild if I stood too close for too long. I'd have to try to keep my distance if I wanted to hold on to my humanity. The first thing I noticed was the two unmade beds that took up most of the tiny room. It made me stop and think for just a moment about what it meant that they were both messed up and looked slept in. My beast scented Clay on both beds, so I decided it meant nothing.

"Clay left about two hours ago." Billy Ray shut the door and walked over to the nearest bed. "I told him he needed to talk to you." She sat down and crossed her legs and arms, closing herself off.

"He came home. That's why I'm here." I didn't make a move to sit, instead I paced, but kept my eyes on Billy Ray. "Why did you tell him he needed to talk to me?" I had my suspicions but hoped that Billy Ray would come right out and tell me they'd fucked.

"Because he's fucked up in the head about you, and that's probably your fault for not explaining things to him the way they needed to be explained." Billy Ray's shoulders relaxed when I stopped walking back and forth and stood staring at her in disbelief. "He knows nothing about what it means to be a werewolf, and you're supposed to be the one to educate him. I honestly don't know how he's survived this long without learning the pack structure or anything else that makes us what we are."

"Well, at first, he didn't want anything to do with me." I was defensive because Billy Ray had a point. I should have tried harder to teach Clay, but he was so fucking stubborn. The only time he seemed interested in werewolf stuff was when it was tied to my past and something he thought he could use to aggravate me. "And now, I'm not sure he cares about anything but himself." Stepping into the narrow space between the beds, I sat down and put my head in my hands. "He took the first chance he could to find the one person he knew I would have a reaction to him fucking and then went out and did just that."

I heard Billy Ray stand up, but I was busy trying to keep back the angry tears that were threatening to fall, so I was surprised when her hand landed on my back. I knew it was a bad idea to let her get so close to me and liking the little jolt of pleasure from something as simple as a touch on the back made me jerk away.

"Nothing happened between Clay and me." Billy Ray's soft voice made me pull my face out of my hands to look at her. "He kissed me, but then we slept in separate beds."

I wanted so badly to believe her, but I could smell Clay so strongly on both beds that there was no way they'd only kissed. What, did they get up and move to the other bed mid-kiss? "I wish I believed that. I really truly do."

"I'm not going to lie to you, Damian. He crawled into my bed sometime in the middle of the night, and I woke up with him curled around me, but we didn't have sex. I wouldn't do that to you, and I don't think Clay would either."

"Why?"

"Why what?" Her brow furrowed as if she didn't fully understand the question when I thought it was a pretty simple one.

"Why wouldn't you do that to me?" She had the most reason to want to see me unhappy, and if I were in her place, I sure as hell would have fucked the hell out of Clay, or let him fuck me as it was.

Her face softened, and she sighed. "You'll never understand, which is why I never tried to explain what you mean to me." I opened my mouth to tell her I should mean less than dick to her, but she gave me a stern glare to keep me silent. "You don't believe that the mate bond exists for a purpose beyond what your parents have drilled into your head, but I was raised in a place where it was the most sacred of all the legacies for a werewolf."

"But Dante told me your parents disowned you when I left." I pointed out the obvious; if it was so revered, why would her own family not want her—? Mate or not, she still bore the sign.

"Because I failed in my purpose, and the pack now bears the burden of my shame."

"I don't get it. It's just a stupid mate bond, not like us fucking is going to change the world." It was stupid, and I didn't want the pressure that would come with it. I wasn't born to lead, and if Billy Ray mated with me it would trigger much bigger problems on her end. I knew I wasn't strong enough to fight off the challengers for the right to breed Billy Ray if we took that step. She'd always be in danger of being abducted for breeding if there was any indication that her mate was weak. I couldn't live with myself if something happened to Billy Ray because of me.

She reached out and took my hand. I immediately tried to tug away from her, but she held on with an iron grip. "I know you think nature fucked up. That there is no such thing as fate, but I think you're wrong." Her eyes searched my face, but I was keeping my thoughts hidden behind a mask of indifference. "I think maybe everything that's happened so far has had a purpose. You have to admit it's too much of a coincidence that I chose to go to college here when I had a lot of other choices."

"That had nothing to do with fate." I rolled my eyes and once again tried to free my hand. The longer she touched me, the louder the beast inside me rallied for us to claim what was ours. I knew I could fight the beast if I maintained my distance from what it desired so badly.

"I think it was fate, and I think you leaving was part of the plan because it led you to Clay."

I was speechless. How could she think that was a good thing? At the moment, I was cursing the day I'd met Clay and everything that had led up to our meeting just reinforced my feeling that the mate bond was more of a curse than a blessing.

"You look shocked." Billy Ray took the hand she was holding and raised it to her lips. After kissing the back of my hand, she ran her cheek over it, and my beast let out a low rumble. "There's more to the mate bond than just fucking, Damian. I've researched some of the more famous accounts of those who found their mates since you came back. You want to hear something shocking?"

I nodded dumbly because my brain wasn't working too well at that point. My beast made my mind feel like what Clay described as having puppy brain. It was fixated on having Billy Ray as its own and the sooner the better.

"In sixty percent of the accounts recorded, dating all the way back to the first pack that came here from Europe, the couple who had the mate bond were actually a triad." She grinned up at me as she continued to nuzzle my hand. I had no idea what she meant by triad, or why she thought it had any bearing on our situation. When she realized I was confused, she expounded to clear things up. "The mated couple had a third. Some of them were very prominent. I assume the ones who were more powerful, but some hung back in the shadows, and there were only rumors as to their ties to the couple. But now you see, we can have this, and Clay is only another piece of the puzzle falling into place."

"But if it was fated, shouldn't our third have been born a genetic werewolf?" Why that was the one thing that popped into my head mystified me since none of what Billy Ray was saying made sense to me.

"No. I don't know if this is one hundred percent true, but I've read a few studies done by some of the underground scientists, you know the ones the counsel finances to look into adapting human medical technology for us? They've been studying infecteds for years. From the bits and pieces I could find—because they keep everything so fucking secret—the virus that causes lycanthropy reacts to something in the DNA of genetic humans and actually makes them a more perfect specimen. It's my theory that this is why many packs have such harsh rules against infecting humans. They're afraid that if enough humans got infected, they'd take over."

When I tugged, she let go of my hand but then moved closer to me as I thought about what she'd said. So far, I only had experience with two infecteds, and if that was anything to go by, Billy Ray's theory made a lot of sense. Both Pete and Clay were exceptionally strong, and I could see either of them challenging any pack leader and winning the battle. But the thing about threesomes and Clay being fated to get infected to be with me and Billy Ray was a little farfetched for me to really take it seriously.

"I know you ran away because you didn't think you'd be able to keep me safe."

Startled out of my thoughts, I turned my head to look at Billy Ray, who was inching her way closer and closer to me on the bed. "That's only part of why I left."

She nodded. "The other part is your family's lust to get back on top, and I get that it's scary, but maybe we can think of a way around that if we put our heads together." With those words, she literally brought our heads together in a soft kiss that ignited a fire in my chest. My beast growled, and I lunged at Billy Ray, pinning her under me on the bed.

After a few more rough kisses, I pulled away from her willing lips to look down at her. I noticed the flush of arousal on her face and how it made her even more alluring, and my beast's chanting grew louder. I struggled to back my beast off for a moment, because although I knew we were too far gone, I needed to make sure Billy Ray was absolutely positive she wanted what was about to happen. Beastly instincts notwithstanding, I was a gentleman. "If we do this, there's no going back. You know that, right?"

Billy Ray nodded her head solemnly. "I know, but I also know this is right." She lifted her hand and palmed the side of my face while staring into my eyes. "I know you don't love me, Damian, but I think if you just give me a chance, you'll come to it eventually, and I'm willing to wait for you to look at me the way you look at Clay. I want that so badly my chest aches when I see you two together."

I'd never thought about how my being with Clay was affecting Billy Ray until I thought Clay had slept with her. I realized I wanted both of them. It may have been for different reasons than Billy Ray's fantasies about the mate bond, but that hardly seemed to matter any longer. I knew my beast wouldn't let me leave because we'd gone too far. It would fight me for its right to claim what belonged to us, and I knew that was what drove people with the unfulfilled mate bond to the brink of insanity. My beast had gotten a taste of what it desired, and there was no denying it now.

"I'm sorry I hurt you, Billy Ray. I'm going to try to do better from now on." I meant it, but there was no way I could promise she wouldn't get hurt when Clay found out what I'd done.

Her smile was sweet when it graced her full lips, but the tears running down the sides of her head to the sheet below didn't escape my attention. I felt like a jackass and opened my mouth to apologize one more time, but she put a finger to my lips to keep me from saying the words.

"Don't tell me. Show me."

Did the human part of me know that I was about to really fuck up my relationship with Clay? Yes. Yes, it did. But did that part of my brain win out? No. No, it didn't. "Tell me you have lube."

"In my bag, over on the chair."

I slid down Billy Ray's body and stood. She followed, but only so she could sit and pull her shirt over her head to reveal the ruby-red camisole underneath. My cock got even harder at the sight. I'd always loved a man in something slinky, but I knew Clay wasn't someone I could ask to indulge that fantasy. Tearing my eyes off the clingy fabric on Billy Ray's chest, I went to the bag and dug through until I found the bottle of lube buried at the bottom. I can't lie; finding the lube under everything else in the bag made my heart a little lighter. I was almost sure Billy Ray hadn't lied when she'd told me she and Clay hadn't done anything, but at the same time it made me rethink what I was about to do.

"Damian?"

I stared down at the lube in my hand and wondered what Clay was doing right then.

"Are you okay?"

The bed creaked and footsteps told me Billy Ray was coming over to where I stood, but still I didn't turn around to face her. She wrapped her arm around my waist and pressed her body tightly against mine so I could feel how turned on she was. My beast rose as I closed my eyes and let her scent wash over me. Fuck, I was so fucked.

"You're having second thoughts, but your wolf knows what it wants. I think for once in your life you should listen to it." Her hand crept down and shoved its way under the waistband of my sweats. I cursed that it had been laundry day because the stretchy material gave her total access to my hard-on, and once she had it in hand, all was lost. My hips bucked as she slowly stroked my cock. "I've been dreaming about this. About how you'd feel in my hand, my mouth, my ass." Her breath ghosted across my neck and raised gooseflesh on my arms.

Turning, and therefore making her release my cock, I stared down into Billy Ray's eyes that were so full of emotion and that cinched the deal for me. I pulled her against me and sealed my lips over hers as I backed her into the nearest bed. My hands found the button on her jeans, and after that, the soft satiny panties she was wearing. Her hard cock strained the limits of the lacy undergarments, but I knew they weren't long for this world when my beast took over. The sound of silk ripping made Billy Ray gasp, but then she stood there bared for my hungry eyes to devour. Looking wasn't enough. I fell to my knees, and took her length into my mouth, making her moan obscenely loud.

She wasn't as long as Clay but just a hair thicker. The moment the thought entered my mind—trying to compare the two of them—I shut it down and just let what came naturally take over. Billy Ray didn't let me stay on my knees for long. She yanked at my hair hard enough that I let out a yelp and glared up at her indignantly.

"I love that you want to do that, but I've waited so long for you that you're just teasing me now." She raised the camisole over her head and threw it to the side. "It's time for you to fuck me." She crawled onto the bed to lie in the center. She looked like a model for some beefcake magazine, and my beast's chant to claim her grew too insistent for me to ignore, no matter how much I wanted to just stand there and gaze at Billy Ray.

"You've really changed, haven't you?" I pushed my sweatpants off and then my ratty old T-shirt before climbing onto the bed.

"Not so much, really." Billy Ray ran her fingers down her chest and over her smooth abs to grab her cock. "Just in the physical sense, actually. I'm still the same geeky guy you left pining for you."

That hurt, and I knew I needed to make it up to her. "Let me prep you." She nodded eagerly and spread her legs to give me access. I grabbed a pillow and shoved it under her hips. With lube-slicked fingers I made sure her ass was well prepared before lubing my cock and sliding up between her thighs, leaving a trail of kisses in my wake that made her clutch at my head.

"I want you to make love to me." She said earnestly but then caught the surprised look on my face. "Or just fuck me if that's what you want."

"No, I want it to be more, too, but I'm not sure how to do it that way." I'd only ever thought it was more than fucking when I'd first started out with Blaine, but after all that had happened with him, I now realized that maybe I'd never done anything other than fuck any of the men I'd been with. Well, maybe not with Clay, but that was one-sided on my part, so I didn't think it counted.

Billy Ray grabbed my face between her hands and lifted her head off the pillow to kiss me gently on the lips before pulling back. "Someday we'll get there. It doesn't have to be today. Today, I just want the wait to be over."

It was my turn to kiss her, and as I did so, I pressed my cock against her entrance. She moaned into my mouth as I breached her and that was the end for me. I don't remember anything from that point on because my beast took over. Hooking Billy Ray's legs over my arms, I drilled into her with only the thought that I needed to claim her for my own, and the only way to do that was to leave a piece of myself inside her. My fangs elongated and the howl that left me when I came was anything but human and was joined by that of Billy Ray as she painted our stomachs with come.

My vision blurred as my arms gave out, and I flopped down on top of Billy Ray. When I tried to roll off, she wrapped her arms around me and held me tight. Our hearts took up the same rhythm. Now the bond between us was so strong, I wondered how I'd ever managed to live without Billy Ray. But as the high of my orgasm started to dissipate, my thoughts turned to how I was going to explain everything to Clay. If this might be the thing that drove him out of my life, because god knew, he never was one to listen before he acted.

Chapter Ten

BILLY RAY

"Mmm, you smell like apples and cinnamon." The murmured words came from behind me as Damian rocked his hips.

We'd passed out and slept after going three rounds the day before, and when I cracked open my eyes, bright light was seeping in under the blackout curtains. I was hungry because we'd only managed to eat some snacks I had in my bag, but I wasn't going to stop Damian when he woke up wanting to have sex. He was taking me slowly this time because the beasts had been satiated and backed off. I was amazed at how it felt to be so intimately linked to another, realizing that the unconsummated mate bond was nothing compared to one that had been fulfilled. If I'd pined for Damian when separated from him before this, I knew I'd wither and die without him now.

"You're probably just starving. I know I am." But I knew he was scenting the change in me, and I smiled because it was so easy to be with werewolves who didn't need to be told how I was feeling.

"I am, but I'm pretty sure your scent would be delicious even if I wasn't." He rolled us over until I was flat on my stomach—my swollen cock trapped between the mattress and my stomach—and he was spread out over my back. His hips only lost their rhythm for a moment, and then they were back to that slow smooth motion that was driving me insane.

Reaching back, I gripped his hip. "Faster, please, just a little faster and harder." He complied, and between him hitting that magical lump of nerves inside me and the friction his movements were causing, I came with a howl. He followed shortly after, landing hard on my back and nuzzling my neck as his breath slowed before rolling off to the side.

He ran his hand through my hair, and I turned to look at him. He grinned. "I'm not sure I'll get used to looking at you with two of the same-colored eyes." I knew what he meant. It was startling to see his green eyes looking back at me, but the real shocker had come when I'd looked in the mirror the previous night, and my own blue eyes stared back at me—both of them. He removed his hand and stretched. "What time is it?"

I reached over and grabbed my phone. "Fuck, it's almost noon. We have to get up. Checkout is in twenty minutes." Rolling over, I sat up. I needed a shower before I could get dressed, but I'd have to hurry if I was going to make checkout.

"Fuck is right." Damian was staring at his own phone. "Clay's going to be pissed. He didn't even try to call or text me, which means he's already too mad to talk to me." He swiped at the screen before holding the phone to his ear.

"I'm going to shower quick." He didn't even look at me or acknowledge I'd said anything. Instead, he stood and paced as he waited for Clay to answer. I closed the bathroom door and showered as quickly as I could, thinking Damian would probably want to take one too. I was right, and he came in just as I was toweling off. I looked at him expectantly for an update on the Clay situation. Clay wasn't going to be happy with the latest development, but I held out hope that Damian would be able to talk to him and make him see that this was going to be the best thing for all three of us in the long run.

"He's not answering. I'm sure he probably drank himself into a coma." Damian tried to smile, but I could see the worry in his eyes as he stepped past me and into the tub. "We'll find out when we get to the RV." He closed the curtain and turned on the water, but his words made me think of all the things that needed to be worked out. It wasn't like I could just run off with Damian and Clay.

"I think I should go back home first." I needed to get a few things, and I didn't think it was proper for me to just disappear on the Maccons after all they'd done for me.

Damian poked his head out, shampoo running down the sides of his head as he did. "I think that's a spectacularly bad idea."

"I have to at least get my personal documents, my computer, and a few other things. I'll be fine. Your family would never hurt me. You know that, and now with proof that we've"—I gestured to my eyes instead of saying fucked—"I'm sure they'll be even more protective of me."

Narrowing his eyes, he opened his mouth to say something, but then a rivulet of soap ran into one of his eyes, and he cursed before disappearing behind the curtain once again. I didn't care what he said. There were things at the Maccon house that I wanted to take with me, and if I was being totally honest, I kind of wanted to avoid being there when Damian told Clay what had happened. I didn't know Clay well, but after spending some time with him, I knew he didn't have a good hold on his beast. While that was normal for werewolves in their first year, most first year werewolves were just young teenage kids who could be controlled by the much stronger adults around them.

I moved out into the room and got dressed as I waited for him to finish showering. Time was ticking, and the guy who worked the desk on the weekends was a total tool who would charge me for an extra night if I didn't check out on time. I was anxious to leave so he wouldn't get the satisfaction. Damian came out with a towel wrapped around his waist. Suddenly time didn't seem to matter as I watched him drop the towel and slide into his sweatpants and then his T-shirt. I still couldn't believe that he was there, and we'd finally done it.

"I still don't feel right about letting you go out to the house alone." He shoved his feet into his sneakers and stood there waiting for a response.

"I can handle myself, and I think you should go to Clay right away. I'll just grab some stuff and head out to the RV park. I'll text you when I'm close."

A frown line creased his brow, and he bit the corner of his lip as he thought. "You know I could make you do what I want, right?" I nodded and then looked down at my feet to show him I knew who was the boss, but I hoped he wouldn't make me go with him. "Fine. Go, but be quick about it. You don't need to pack anything you can easily replace. Just tell them you're going to stay with me at the camper for a bit, sorta like a honeymoon period before we decide what we're doing."

The grin on my face was huge, and I felt all giddy at him using the word honeymoon, but then his serious expression wiped my smile away. "Okay, got it. Lie my ass off and then get the hell out of there before they figure out you're never coming back."

"Right. And if you're not at the camper in"—he looked at his phone—"two hours, I'm coming to find you and things will get messy."

"Give me three hours because of the drive, and you know your mom will want some details. If I try to rush it too much, she'll get suspicious." He knew I was right and nodded. "We need to go, or Jack down in the office will charge me for another night." I grabbed my bag, ready to go, but when I tried to walk past Damian, he pulled me into his arms.

"Just be safe, okay? I'm still not sure about this shit, but now I know if something happens to you, I'm going to lose it." He stared down into my eyes until I agreed with a nod, and then he kissed me softly before letting me go. "Let's go get this done."

I'D HAD ANOTHER reason for wanting to leave the motel as quickly as possible. It being Sunday, I knew the Maccons would be at the weekly pack potluck held in the basement of the church on the compound, which would give me time to pack some bags and load them in my Jeep without them seeing me do it. It was also the reason I'd asked for the extra hour. I did want to let the family know I was going to be with Damian. They already worried about Damian, and I didn't see the need to add to their strife with my disappearance.

After parking in the drive, I let myself into the house and made my way up to my bedroom. I wasted no time in pulling out two large duffels and packing the stuff I thought I couldn't live without. Damian told me to leave my clothes, but there were some pieces that held special meaning to me, and I didn't want to leave them behind.

I'd just zipped up the second bag when the front door slammed shut, and I heard voices. First I thought about hiding my bags in the closet, but then how would I get them out? Sliding open the glass patio doors that led to a small balcony, I stepped out and dropped the bags over the edge. They were on the side of the house where I hoped no one would notice them or me when I went to grab them after making my excuse to leave. I was back at my bed with a smaller bag half packed when Linda opened the door after giving a warning tap.

Her eyes searched the room before landing on me. I thought for sure I was caught, but then she turned and hollered out the door for David and Dante. I stood as still as a statue, not turning around until I knew the two men had joined her. When I did, Linda's hand flew to her mouth, and both David and Dante's jaws dropped.

"Is he here?" Linda once again swept the room with her gaze before returning to staring at me.

"No, he's not, and he's not coming yet." I held up my hand to stop all three of them when they looked ready to start arguing with me. "He wants me to come to the RV park and spend a little time with him. Sort of like a honeymoon." I looked down as the heat rose up my neck. It was a lie, but even the thought made me blush.

Linda was the first to come into the room and wrap her arms around me. "I'm so happy for you, Billy Ray. I knew my boy would come to his senses sooner or later."

Nodding, I tried to separate myself from her, but she held on tight. "He just needs some time to adjust and figure out what we're going to do."

"What do you mean, what you're going to do?" David's voice finally made Linda release me as she turned to glare at her husband. "He's going to get his ass back here and take his rightful place at the head of the pack, and if he thinks any different, he's got another think coming."

"David, hush, you know Billy Ray will bring him back now that their bond is complete." Linda stepped in to calm the situation, but it was Dante's turn to voice his opinion.

"Damian finally get rid of that mutt then?" Dante scented the air around me, and his pupils dilated.

"If he's with his mate, I'm sure he must have gotten rid of that other one." Linda looked so happy I almost felt bad for lying to her.

"Probably found out that nothing good can come of being with an infected." Dante was slowly inching his way toward me. I didn't like the way he was looking at me, but I trusted David and Linda to step in if Dante couldn't control himself. Of course, I hadn't anticipated their stunned silence when Dante exposed Damian and Clay's secret, so when Dante growled and lunged at me, it was only my nimble feet that kept me out of his clutches.

When I ran into the dresser, it broke David out of his stupor, and he stepped in to restrain his youngest son. "Stand down, boy." David's wolf made his voice deep and growly, and his son went limp in his arms.

"What happened?" Dante looked around as if in a daze.

All the Maccon men were alphas. Even Damian, though he was a special sort who needed a mate to bring him into power, and as alphas they would sense the change in me, and on differing levels, be driven to claim me. I had counted on David's ability to control his beast and his son on behalf of the family. If either one of them got between me and Damian, they'd be forced to fight him for me and one of them wouldn't survive the rumble. I knew David was in no hurry to lose either of his sons, or the chance at once again being the top family which was exactly what would happen if he or Dante defiled the mate bond.

"It's the scent Billy Ray is giving off. It got to your head." David loosened his hold on Dante but didn't let him go completely. "It's okay. The pull is strong, but you can control yourself if you try, and you have to try because if any harm comes to him we'll all pay the price." Dante nodded and swallowed so hard I could hear it. David dropped his arms to his sides, but I could see he was ready to corral Dante again if he got out of control. "Now, what's this about some infected?"

Shit. I'd hoped they'd forget Dante had said that.

"Clay, that guy Damian's with, he's an infected. Damian told me one day when we had coffee that he infected him, and his pack made him take responsibility for Clay. That's why he was here with Damian." Dante looked to me as if he thought I'd corroborate his story, but I was busy taking in how Linda and David received the news.

When they stood there having a silent conversation with their eyes and facial expressions, I knew that everything I'd learned about the infecteds was true, and they knew they'd been perpetuating the lies the whole time. It was a cover-up, and the people who had sheltered me, and who I loved because they'd been there when I'd needed them most were part of the conspiracy.

Linda turned to me and asked, "Did you know about Clay?"

I nodded just as my phone rang. After digging it out of my pocket and seeing it was Damian, I answered it without thinking. "Hello?"

"He's not here!" Damian's shrill raised voice would have carried to the other three people in the room even if they didn't have superior hearing, but there was no way I could tell him to shush without looking suspicious.

"Maybe he went for a walk?" I turned and tried to will Damian to quiet down. Why couldn't he have just texted?

"He took his computer! He wouldn't take his computer on a fucking walk!" I could hear Damian slamming cupboard doors and drawers before he said, "And he packed all his favorite clothes. He's fucking gone, and I have no idea where he went."

"Okay, calm down." I stopped and took a few deep breaths, hoping he'd follow suit. "Y'all only have the one car, right? So it's not like he could have gone far on foot."

"Oh, like he couldn't have called a fucking cab or hitchhiked to the fucking airport." The sarcasm dripped from Damian's words, but I decided to ignore his attitude since I knew he was probably frantic with worry.

"Listen, let me finish up here, and I'll come, and we can look for him, okay?"

"No, I'm going out to see if I can find him. Just call me when you're out of there, and we can meet up." Damian hung up before I could say anything else.

"So, he's not giving up the mutt for you, which means he's not coming back here, right?" Dante was the first to point out the obvious.

"He was going to send him back to the pack so he wasn't out on his own." I lied. I knew they'd know it, but I had to try.

Linda and David huddled together, and their barely breathed words were inaudible from across the room. I didn't like the feeling I was getting and wished I'd have given in to Damian and just gone with him. I was stupid to think I could pull this off. With a look at Dante, they formed a semicircle around me, trapping me against the bed.

"We're going to get Clay out of the way for you, Billy Ray, but you're going to have to help us." David leveled his gaze at me to let me know he would broker no argument.

"I don't know how I can help you. I don't have any idea where he is."

Dante grinned and reached out to snatch my phone out of my hand. There was no use in protesting since they were stronger than me. "Password is DM2012," I said with a sigh. He nodded and then started swiping and poking at my phone while I stood there under the watchful gaze of his parents.

"Ah, here it is." He held the phone up, and what was on the screen made me cringe. "Damian told me how he met that fucker. I figure if he's as pissed as I'd be if my girlfriend stepped out on me, I'd be looking for a comfort fuck."

"Don't be crude." Linda slapped him in the back of the head, but her fond smile told the world how her little man could do no wrong in her eyes.

"Do you know what his user name is?" I shook my head, and Dante started swiping through the app. "No matter, I'm pretty sure you can find him." He stepped in close and held out my phone for me, but not before quirking his lip in a snarl to let me know I better not try anything funny.

I looked at profile pictures. Having no idea how he expected me to find Clay among the thousands of users, I'd give it a shot until I could think of a way to get a message to Damian about his family's plan. I had no idea what they'd do with Clay if they got him, but I was sure they weren't going to welcome him into the family. Nothing good could come of this, and if I could prevent it from happening, I would.

Chapter Eleven

CLAY

It was 4:30 in the afternoon when I woke up, but I wished I could go back to sleep. I wanted the world to disappear and sleep was the perfect way to forget what a damn mess my life was. Unfortunately, I had no luck and instead got up and showered. I ran through my last day and a half—the half being the easy part because I'd spent it passed out—I wasn't happy about how things had turned out.

After Damian left, I'd packed my bags, thinking I'd wait for him to come back, so I could storm out, but surprise, surprise, he never came home. I waited until it was almost dark, then headed to the highway to see if I could catch a lift into town. I had no idea what I was going to do but knew if I was home when Damian got there nothing good would come of it. I'd gotten lucky when the guy who'd picked me up the day before pulled up behind me and offered me a ride again. I endured his comments about making this a habit, and not knowing where else to go, I had him drop me off at the Royal Inn.

Imagine my surprise when Damian's truck was sitting there in the parking lot right next to Billy Ray's Jeep. I asked the desk clerk for the room across from the one I'd spent the previous night in, which he happily gave me. After dropping off my bags, I went to the bar, ate a greasy burger, and got the bartender to sell me two bottles of vodka before trudging back. I had to stop myself from going up the opposite set of stairs and knocking down the door. Instead I paced in front of the window, looking for signs of life from the room across the way. When full dark fell, there was no sign that they were even in there—no small strip of light around the window like normal. I wondered if maybe they'd gone somewhere as I cracked open the first bottle.

Sometime around eleven, and half a bottle in, a howl reached my ears. It was faint but unmistakably Damian's. My hackles rose and my beast made my chest vibrate with its answering rumble. I knew then that what I'd had with Damian was over, but my beast wasn't one to be detoured so easily. I quickly downed the last half of the vodka, hoping I'd pass out, but though the blackness was there on the edge of my vision, it hung just out of reach.

I'd fucked up. I'd taken too long to figure out my feelings for Damian weren't just a product of my beast's lust, and now I'd lost him. Not one to cry, I downed some more alcohol and then buried my head beneath the pillow before passing out.

After wrapping a towel around my waist, I stepped out of the bathroom while rubbing at my hair with a hand towel. I went straight for the window. Peering out at the parking lot, my stomach dropped when both vehicles were gone from where they'd been parked the previous day. So they'd left. I checked my phone. There were many missed calls and texts from Damian, but they hadn't come until after noon which meant he hadn't even given me a thought until he'd left the motel. Fuck him. I wasn't going to read his messages because part of me knew once I did, it would officially be over.

I found the number for a pizza place, and called in an order as I opened the second bottle of vodka and lounged back on the bed. I had to figure out what I was going to do. Maybe I should just go back home, but if I did, what would I do for work? On the other hand, I couldn't really stay because that meant having to see Damian every day, and Billy Ray when I went to pick up my paystub. Neither of my options seemed like good ones, and then it hit me that I would also be a lone wolf now that I was no longer with Damian. Fuck, my life sucked on so many levels.

Needing something to clear my head, because alcohol wasn't doing it for me, I pulled up the Grindr app on my phone and started swiping through the available men in my area. Getting off always gave me a better outlook on life, and now that I wasn't attached to anyone, I was free to find a hookup for the night. Not that I couldn't have before, but why go looking when I had a warm and willing body around? A sharp knock on the door startled me just as I thought I'd found a good prospect. I'd have ignored it, but I was sure it was my food. The way my stomach was growling told me I'd better eat soon or else.

As I paid for my food, my Grindr app message alert sounded. I thanked the delivery guy and threw my two pizzas on the table before going for my phone. A user named southerncountriboi sent me a message. I looked at his picture, which was obviously not a pic of him, since it was a well-known actor, and I almost swiped to decline but then...shit. It wasn't like there were many prospects out there on a Sunday night, and his profile did say he liked to suck cock. Why not?

[looking for a good time?] Not very original, but then neither was using someone famous for your profile pic.

It only took a few seconds for southerncountriboi to respond. Someone was eager. *[m always looking for a good time. u got somewhere we can meet?]*

Yep, eager, but so was I. I needed something to drive the images of Damian and Billy Ray fucking all night out of my mind. *[you know where the Royal Inn is?]*

[who doesn't know where the Royal Inn is?]

[Room 201 hurry up]

[b there in a jiff]

Frowning at his choice of words, I typed one more reply to tell him I'd be waiting, before throwing my phone onto the bed and descending on the pizza. I needed fuel, or I'd be too worn out to have any fun. I'd devoured almost one whole pie when knocking at my door startled me. Man, that boi didn't lie when he'd said he'd be there in a jiff. Looking longingly at the other untouched pizza, I got up. We could always eat it as a snack after the first round if the guy was any good, and if not, I could eat it alone once I'd sent him on his way.

After wiping my hands and mouth on one of the hotel hand towels, I went to answer the door. I should have looked out the peephole. Why the fuck didn't I look out the goddamn-fucking peephole?

COMING AROUND—CHAINED up and blindfolded—I cursed. Seriously? Who the hell gets kidnapped twice? Fuck. Fucking Damian. If he was behind this again, I was going to kill that motherfucker. I twisted, testing my bonds to see if there was any way to get free, but right away, I knew whoever had shackled me to whatever I was chained to had meant business. There were no padded handcuffs or soft ropes this time; instead, cold hard steel encircled my wrists and bare ankles. No way out without a key. I was fucked.

I turned my other senses loose. Not being able to see was a much bigger handicap before I'd contracted lycanthropy, but now I could smell and hear way better. First thing I noticed was that I was alone in the room but not in the structure. I could hear faint voices coming from somewhere not too far from where I was being held but couldn't make out the words. So there was more than just one kidnapping asshole this time and one—I was almost sure—was a woman. Her scent stood out among the others my sensitive nose detected. The sound of the door opening made me freeze but pretending to still be unconscious didn't work.

"Stop pretending. We could hear the change in your breathing the minute you came to." It was a deep masculine voice. It wasn't Damian's, but I'd be damned if it wasn't similar.

"What do you want from me? I'm nobody, and no one is going to pay you to set me free." What other reason could people have for kidnapping someone?

"Just keep your mouth closed and sit still. When we get what we want, you'll be free to go." A different voice this time, still masculine and still so damn unnervingly like Damian's. Then it hit me.

"You must be Dante, right?" One of them had to be the brother and the other the father, maybe? But what did they have to gain by locking me up?

"I said shut your mouth." A hard kick to my thigh gave me a cramp that I couldn't even try to soothe out because my hands were above my head. I hissed instead and tried to relax my leg muscles.

"Don't hurt him." Oh, well now, that was a voice I recognized. Even if I'd never heard Billy Ray use that tone—the one that held the threat of death—and even though I was wriggling in pain, I would still know his voice anywhere.

"Et tu, Billy Ray?"

"What the fuck language you speaking?" Dante—it had to be him—landed another kick, this time connecting with my knee and making me howl in pain.

"I said stop it." Billy Ray's voice preceded the sound of a scuffle. I grinned through the pain at the thought of Billy Ray defending me. What a dumb ass. He had Damian. What did he care what they did to his castoff?

"That's enough!" It was the female's turn to get into the fray. "You two boys stop that fighting, and you"—there was a pause, and I could only imagine why—"don't kick him anymore. We need him in good shape, or you know who might not do what he's supposed to do."

I snorted behind the bag that served as my blindfold. "You know who doesn't give a shit about me, and if you think he does, you're fucking delusional. Just ask the guy he fucked all night last night. Right, Billy Ray?" Okay, I was still more than a little pissed about that.

"Clay, if you would have just answered your phone, none of this would be happening." Billy Ray was close to me as he spoke, and all I could think of was punching him for fucking my man. Fucking handcuffs made it impossible, but I'd remember the feeling, and as soon as I was free, Billy Ray had better watch his back.

"Get over here and make the call." The other male voice barked.

They didn't even bother leaving the room this time. I guess since they knew that I knew who they were, there was no point in trying to hide their plans from me. I sat there, my knee and thigh both white hot balls of pain and listened to Billy Ray's end of the conversation.

"Damian, it's me. I found Clay." He paused. "No, we're not at the RV. We're at the hunting cabin. Can you get here as quick as you can, please?" The wheedling note in his voice should have tipped Damian off that something wasn't right. "Please, just come as fast as you can."

"Damian, get your ass out here right the fuck now." I wasn't sure if Dante had snatched the phone away, or if he was just hollering it at Billy Ray.

"Yes, Dante's here with me." Billy Ray paused again, and this time I could make out some of Damian's angry words. He was not happy to say the least. "Yes, they're here too. You know what that means. If you don't come soon, I can't promise nothing bad will happen to Clay. I know you love him too much to let him get hurt. Hurry, Damian."

My mind was reeling. Either Billy Ray wasn't a willing participant in this kidnapping, or he was a damn convincing actor. I was still lost as to what Damian's family thought they had to gain by holding me. He'd chosen his bonded mate, which meant I was no one, just like I'd told them earlier because no matter what Billy Ray said, Damian obviously didn't love me.

The sound of footsteps and the door closing made me think I was alone, but then a warm body sat down next to me and a hand settled on my bare arm. "I'm sorry. I had no idea they were going to do this, or I wouldn't have gone home." Billy Ray squeezed my forearm.

"I don't understand why."

He knew exactly what I was talking about without me having to specify what part of the deal I didn't understand so explained it to me. "They want Damian to come home, but he was going to leave. He never planned on coming back to the pack."

That made even less sense after what I'd heard in the motel. "But you two—you fucked last night, and that means you're bonded now, right?"

His breath caught in his chest when confronted with me knowing the truth of what they'd done. "I'm sorry. I never meant to hurt you, but if you'd just agree to listen, Damian and I have a plan."

Shaking my head, I didn't want to listen to any of their plans that probably didn't include me as anything other than a friend. "I don't care what you and Damian do. From here on out, I'm a lone wolf unless I find a pack that isn't fucked-up like yours and the other one we were in before." Slim hope there. Seemed like every pack had its own problems, and I doubted I'd ever find one that would accept an infected into their ranks.

"You don't understand. There's a place for a wolf like you and we—"

"Billy Ray, get your ass out here!"

"You better go. Your in-laws are calling, and they don't seem like the sort who like to be kept waiting." I turned my head away, showing him I was through with discussing anything further.

"I won't let them hurt you, and when Damian gets here, we'll leave, all of us, together." Billy Ray stood after giving me what I'm sure he thought was a reassuring pat on the arm. I tracked his footsteps to the door, then let my head fall forward. I wouldn't cry, not over being kidnapped, and damn well not over a man who chose someone else.

IT'S NOT EASY to keep track of time in a hood. It could have been minutes or hours before I heard the commotion in the other room, which I figured meant Damian had arrived. Then the door banged open, and what sounded like a fight entered the room I was being held in.

"You can't just fucking kidnap someone!" Oh, that was rich coming from Damian. I almost laughed but figured it was the wrong time for it.

"If you'd calm down and listen for once instead of going off half-cocked, maybe we could have worked things out without resorting to this." The female, who I was sure was Damian's mom, sounded just like Damian when he'd said those words to me.

"Maybe I don't give a shit about what you have to say. You ever think about that?"

"You have an obligation to this family and to the pack. You can't keep shirking the responsibility because you don't like the idea of being in charge. You're a Maccon, my heir, and once you step up, the rightful leader of this pack." Damian's father sounded like a supreme douche nozzle. I would have run away if he'd been my dad too.

"I'm not your property! You don't own your kids, and since I'm over the legal age of consent, I don't have to do anything but what I want to do. Where are the fucking keys for these handcuffs?" Another skirmish and I wondered how far they were willing to go with this kidnapping thing if Damian didn't give into their wishes. I didn't have to wait long to find out.

Yanked to my feet, which were chained together, I stumbled at the abrupt change in position, but then an arm was around my neck, keeping me from falling back to the floor. "Sit down and listen to Mom and Dad, or I'll choke the life out of this mutt, then break his neck for good measure."

Growls filled the room, and I realized mine was the loudest among them. The arm around my neck tightened and that only served to piss off my beast. The funny thing is I knew shifting wouldn't actually improve my situation, since I wasn't yet a full-grown wolf, but once the beast got that close to the surface, I was powerless to stop it.

Problem was, I couldn't hit my own mother, no matter how badly she deserved it right then. I went for Dante, who had Billy Ray's right arm pulled up behind his back, restraining him while my mother got to her feet. I managed to get there just as she was getting ready to knee Billy Ray in the balls. Grabbing her leg, I flipped her back onto the bed and only had to reach down and grab one of the sets of handcuffs to secure her, but Dante kicked them out of my reach.

It was Billy Ray who changed the course of the fight. Bringing his head back, he broke Dante's nose with the back of his skull. Bloodied and howling, Dante let go of Billy Ray's arm, and my mate jumped into action. He threw me a set of handcuffs while grabbing the other set for himself. I handcuffed my mother to the bed while he cuffed my father's hands behind his back. Then I went to check on Clay. Pulling the rope from his neck, I threw it to Billy Ray who used it to bind Dante's hands. I picked up Clay's small form and sighed in relief when I felt his normal fast breathing.

"You're choosing a mutt over your own flesh and blood." Dante hissed the words at me before spitting out a mouthful of blood.

"No, I'm choosing a man I love over people who only want to use me." I hugged Clay to my chest as Billy Ray stood. "Let's go, Billy Ray." I wanted to go, hook up the camper, and put as much space between me and my family as I could. Now that they finally realized I wasn't coming back, they would probably blow the whistle on the infected in the pack's territory as soon as they got free, and that would spell trouble for the three of us.

"Damian!" My mother's angry voice stopped me in my tracks, much like it did when I was younger and in for a whupping. "Don't leave like this. We only wanted to talk to you and taking Clay was the only way to get you to listen to us."

Turning, I glared down at the woman who'd given birth to me but whom I no longer considered my mom. "Maybe you could have just called?"

"Like you would have listened over the phone. Always so goddamn stubborn, never listening to anyone who had a different take on life than you." My father had managed to roll over and sit up so he could train his eyes on me. His beast was so close I could smell it, and I knew he was holding on to it with only the sheer will of his humanity because I was doing the same.

"Your take on life is only to have as much power as you can get. It's time for the Maccons to get over losing the pack leadership to the Luptons and move on. I'm not going to be your heir or your tool to bring your fantasy to life." I turned to look at Billy Ray, who gave me a single nod. He understood now why I'd had to leave all those years ago.

Clay stirred in my arms and let out a low growl as if he was remembering what happened right before he passed out and was pissed as hell about it. I petted his head and held him close. I supposed we were in for another weird time while his body figured out how to deal with another unexpected shift. Not like I expected Clay to do anything by the rules, but did he have to break every single one of them?

"You really do love him, huh?" Dante's nose was still bleeding profusely though it was probably well on its way to being healed. I felt a pang of sadness over losing my baby brother.

"Yeah, I do, and I'm disappointed in you. I never would have taken you for someone who would treat a person like you did Clay. I'm sorry to say this, but I no longer consider you my family either." I looked from my brother's stricken face to my parents, who were glaring daggers at me.

"We should get out of here." Billy Ray stepped in close and put his hand on my back, gently turning me away from my family. I let him guide me out to the truck where he opened the passenger door and made me get in with Clay before slipping behind the wheel. "I figured it was better if I drove so you could check Clay for any injuries." He started the engine and turned on the lights so I could see him by the glow from the dashboard.

I reached out and touched his shoulder to get him to look at me. "Thank you." I didn't know how to tell him how much it meant to me that he'd helped me save Clay, even though he knew my feelings for him.

"It's fine. I don't mind driving." He pulled out onto the gravel track that served as the cabin's driveway.

"That's not what I meant, and you know it."

He nodded. "Yeah, I know, but I don't know exactly how to tell you it was partially my fault. If I hadn't insisted on going back to the house, they never would have gotten to Clay. They made me use the Grindr app to set up a date with him."

I rolled Billy Ray's words around in my head, but still I couldn't lay the blame on his shoulders when I knew he was more than willing to try to make some sort of relationship between the three of us work. "When we get some miles between us and the pack's territory, all three of us are deleting that goddamn app. It's nothing but fucking trouble." I looked down at Clay, who gave one sharp bark that I'd like to think was agreement but probably wasn't. "I don't think he suffered any injuries."

"Yeah, he was lucky he shifted. I think it made Linda less willing to hurt him even if she was saying differently." Billy Ray pulled out on the highway and hit the gas. He was speeding a little, but I wasn't going to tell him to slow down because I knew Dante would break free from the ropes within minutes of our leaving. I wouldn't put it past any of them to give chase.

"I think she'd still have killed him. What the hell were they thinking?" It all seemed a bit much, kidnapping and attempted murder? I'd never have thought my family was capable of such darkness.

Billy Ray sighed. "You want to know what they'd planned?" His hands tightened on the steering wheel.

"I don't know. Do I?"

"They were going to offer to let Clay go free if you stayed with me and the pack."

"That's it? That was the whole plan?" Seemed overly simple to me.

"No, they weren't really going to release Clay. I think they planned to make it look like they did, but then they were going to get rid of him because they heard you on the phone when you couldn't find him. They knew you wouldn't give up that easily, and even if you agreed to stay, you'd bolt at the first chance you got to go to him."

Looking down at Clay who was napping with his head lying on my thigh, I knew my family was right. Even with the completed mate bond, I felt drawn to Clay in a way I didn't think I could ignore. I scratched his head, and he snuffled in his sleep. "I shouldn't have let you go. I'm responsible for you now, and I fucked up not keeping you with me." Thoughts of someone trying to claim Billy Ray, now that he was in full power, reminded me of how I felt about Clay. It was weird being pulled in two different directions at once. I felt like I'd never find peace of mind again.

"Do you think he'll shift back?" Billy Ray spared a glance at Clay before returning his attention to the road.

"I really don't know. Last time he shifted when he wasn't supposed to be able to, it was from pup to human, and then his brain wasn't right. Then he shifted to pup form for an entire month. I was worried out of my mind, but he was fine in the end." I shrugged, figuring nature would once again take its course.

"He's so powerful. I didn't really believe all the stuff I found on infecteds when I was researching the mate bond, but seeing Clay, I can't deny it's true now."

We pulled into the RV park, and I directed Billy Ray to our camper. It was going to take a lot of work to get us loaded and out of there. Clay woke up, and when I opened the door he jumped out of the truck. Too bad he wasn't in his human shape, we could have used the extra set of hands.

"You get all the outdoor stuff packed up while I retract the pop outs. If you want to start loading stuff into the storage underneath, I'll handle unhooking everything when I'm done." Billy Ray nodded and started picking up chairs and other stuff we'd put outside to use when the weather wasn't shitty. We probably could have left most of the stuff and just bought replacements, but it was going to take me some time to get the pop outs in and the trailer unhooked, so I figured Billy Ray may as well keep busy and out of my way.

Clay followed me inside where the cats hissed at him, and he barked back until I hollered at him to shut up and kenneled the felines. Retracting the pop outs seemed to take forever, but once they were all in I went out and around the back where the electrical and sewer hookups were. Before I could disconnect everything, Clay stood at attention, with his hackles raised, growling. I stopped and stilled and that was when I heard voices coming from the front. Clay took off in a run, and I followed, trusting his instincts that something wasn't right.

Pulling up short, I grabbed for Clay before one of the men standing in our lot could punt him with the heavy steel-toed boots he was wearing. There were six of them, and two were holding Billy Ray by the arms while one stood over him. I recognized the back of that head. Having stared at it for most of my high school days, there was no mistaking him. "Don't do anything stupid. They'll kill you before you have a chance to get one bite in." I warned Clay off attacking because he had no chance against them.

"What are you doing here, JR?" I addressed the leader of the gang. JR Lupton, the son of the pack leader, smirked as he turned to face me, leaving his buddies to restrain Billy Ray.

"Well, well, well, looky who we got here, boys." When he took a step in my direction, two of the others flanked him. "If it isn't Damian Maccon. The prodigal son has returned. Too bad his mamma and pappy don't want him no more." His buddies snickered like he'd said something funny.

That cleared up why they'd come. Someone in my family thought it was a good idea to call the pack on me, and now I would face pack justice since I'd violated their law about infecteds. But I wasn't going to go down without a fight. "We were actually just getting ready to leave. So if you'd call off your goons"—I looked past him to where Billy Ray was struggling against the hold of two much bigger men—"we'll be on our way."

The smirk on JR's face turned down into a frown, and he lifted his trucker hat to scratch his head. "Well, you see, I'd like to let you be on your way as you say, but thing is, you're trying to abduct a member of my pack, and I can't let that happen. I have a duty to protect even the lowliest members." He looked back at Billy Ray. "Ain't that right, Billy Ray? You need my protection, just like back in the old days when I made sure that nobody took advantage of you when you passed out drunk in one of them pretty little dresses you like to wear."

My chest vibrated with a low growl at the thought of Billy Ray with JR *fucking* Lupton. I sent my mate a heated glare that he quickly turned away from in shame.

"Oh, he never told you about that, huh? How me and him used to mess around a little after you left?" JR's smirk was back. "Yeah, I figured he wouldn't tell you. Wouldn't want you to know he had a real man to compare you to."

That was it. I charged JR, even though I knew I wasn't going to win this fight. He had us outnumbered, and with Clay being in no shape to help, we were fucked. It didn't stop me, and it surprised everyone else so much that I managed to take JR to the ground before any of the others reacted. It didn't take long for them to fall on me, though, and as soon as I was dragged off JR, they began kicking and hitting me. Three against one, with Clay nipping at their heels, wasn't good odds, and when JR got up to join in, hell, I was just hoping for a quick death.

"Leave him alone, JR, and I'll go with you willingly." Billy Ray's voice stopped at least one pair of fists as JR stood up and motioned for the other three to stop too. "I'll go with you and be yours if you let Damian and Clay go."

"What are you talking about?" Looking up at Billy Ray from my position on the ground, and through the rapid closing of my left eye, I tried to read what was going on in his head. Why would JR want him to...? "Oh, fuck no!" I tried to get to my feet, but the goons wouldn't let me, and I ended up just struggling against them in vain.

"It's for the best." Billy Ray looked resigned to his fate, but there was no way I was going to let them take my mate.

"Listen to Billy Ray, Damian. He was always so much smarter than you. Went to college and everything." JR left me to walk over to Billy Ray. He grabbed Billy Ray's jaw and forced him to look into his face. "You're no country bumpkin. Not one of us uneducated hicks; you're smart enough to know that hitching your wagon to the future pack leader is a much better bet than trailing after a loser Maccon. Mate bond or no, he's never going to be enough man for you. Right, sweetheart?" Leaning in, JR rubbed his nose along Billy Ray's jaw and growled possessively.

Clay, who I'd all but forgotten when the fighting started, barked and lunged at JR. JR dispatched Clay easily with a boot to the chest. With a yelp of pain, Clay fell back to the ground and lay still. I worried that he'd been grievously injured, but then my attention was drawn back to Billy Ray when he yelped but for a wholly different reason.

I thrashed against the arms that turned into bodies holding me down when I saw what JR was doing to my mate. He'd turned Billy Ray around and was grinding up against him.

"I swear I'll kill all of you, motherfuckers!" I gave one last push to get free, but the lugs holding me down started punching me again. One good shot to the solar plexus immobilized me and left me helplessly watching as JR started undoing Billy Ray's pants.

"I think I need to claim you right here in front of Damian so he knows who you belong to."

I couldn't watch. Instead, I looked to where Clay was lying on the ground, and I swear he grinned at me before I closed my eyes.

Chapter Thirteen

CLAY

Oh, I was pissed. First, at my body for betraying me and turning me into a wolf the size of a dog, and second, at those assholes who were beating on Damian, and to round out the top three—who did that fucker think he was, touching Billy Ray like that? After the one Damian called JR kicked me, I played opossum, not wanting to draw any attention to myself while I tried to figure out a way to get the three of us out of the mess we were in. Even if I managed to change back, it was still six against three, making the odds too great in the other team's favor. I was no bookie, but I wouldn't have placed any bet on us.

Damian looked over to me when it was apparent what JR planned to do to Billy Ray, and a half-formed idea started bouncing around my puppy brain. Not able to let it alone once it was there, I chased it like I did my tail. Once I caught it, I tried to smile to let Damian know I had a plan. I forgot dogs can't exactly smile so I winked, hoping he'd get it and be ready to back me up if I managed to do the thing.

Latching on to the feeling in the back of my mind, I concentrated on embracing the change while keeping eye contact with Damian. When he caught on that I was trying to force the change, though he didn't know the form I was aiming to achieve, he looked horrified but also resigned. As it hit, I closed my eyes because this is where it got tricky.

Pete had told me, as infected werewolves, we were special and as such had powers that we kept to ourselves—only telling those closest to us because otherwise the genetic weres would have even more reason to seek our deaths. I was about to see if he was right even though, according to Pete, because I was still a pup, it might be too soon for me to be able to do it.

The change is something indescribable, but the feeling of bones lengthening while the ones in my skull reformed was something straight out of a horror movie. Before the change was complete, I pushed that spark away, stopping it. When I opened my eyes, the look on Damian's face told me I'd been successful. I was a Lycan, and as I stood, the six men who were set on terrorizing the man I loved, and the one my beast insisted on protecting, stared with open-mouthed awe.

I tried to tell them to run before I ripped them to shreds, but my mouth wasn't human enough to form the words and only snarls came out. One of the men, the bravest or stupidest, stepped between me and JR. It only took one swipe of my clawed hand to make him realize it was the dumbest thing he'd ever done as he fell to the ground, clutching the gaping wound I'd made in his chest.

JR stopped trying to rape Billy Ray, and when he turned, I could see what was about to happen. In seconds, he'd transformed into a large black wolf. My chuckle was the thing of children's nightmares, but it didn't deter JR, who leaped at me.

"Clay!" Damian shouted my name, but I couldn't let him distract me from the immediate threat of having my throat ripped out.

JR's strong jaws clamped down on my forearm, and not only did I feel the bone break, but I also heard it. *Better the arm than the neck*, I thought, as I brought my heavily muscled leg up to knee him in the chest, causing him to release my arm as he dropped to the ground. He was down, but not out. The weres in human form joined in the fight, kicking and punching me, giving him time to recover.

A familiar howl from behind me rang into the night air as Damian, in wolf form, jumped one of the two who were still holding Billy Ray. With only one man to deal with, Billy Ray was free within moments after crushing the guys nuts with his knee and then landing a few hard punches to the guy's face. Before he could come to help me fight off the three who were pounding on me, JR cut him off with a snarl. Billy Ray stood staring at the big wolf, and in human form, he was no match for JR. I wasn't sure if he'd be more effective as a wolf, because JR was a huge specimen, but it seemed like that choice wasn't his to make, so it was up to me and Damian to protect him.

I was worried when a truck pulled onto the street, headlights splashing us with light before it jerked to a stop. Reinforcements? Or some unlucky human about to get a huge surprise? I hoped for the latter, while expecting the former, but couldn't take the time to find out when I was fighting for my life.

Turning to one of the guys hitting me, I grabbed him by the neck and squeezed until his eyes bulged out. I wanted to break his neck or tear his throat out but instead threw his limp body at one of his friends when he passed out from lack of oxygen. With that guy dealing with an unconscious body on top of him, I slashed out with my unbroken arm, extending my claws at the third man. He dodged, and I lunged, sinking my sharp teeth into his shoulder and making him scream out in pain. I took a chunk of flesh with me when I withdrew, and the guy went to his knees, watching me with a look of shock on his face as he tried to stem the crimson flow from his wound.

Having dispatched his opponent, Damian had drawn the attention of JR. They were circling each other, as the last guy who I'd been fighting and the one Billy Ray had kneed in the groin, dragged the wounded toward the two pickups sitting on the road in front of our camper. It was now unfairly balanced in our favor, three to one—no, wait, there was another wolf. His coloring was the same as Damian's, and he was pacing in front of Billy Ray, as if he was guarding him. Not deeming the newcomer a threat, I went back to where Damian and JR were still sizing each other up.

Focused on Damian, JR didn't seem to notice how the odds had changed. He attacked Damian, going for the neck. That was all it took. I don't even remember what happened next because all I saw was red as I attacked. When it was over, I dropped the limp body of my opponent to the ground and sank to my knees.

"Clay, are you okay?" Touching my shoulder, Billy Ray startled me, and I snarled at him. He jumped back but then shook his head as if ashamed of his fear. "I know you can understand me. I know you won't hurt me, so I'm going to take a look at that arm. It's hanging funny, and I think it needs to be set before you start healing wrong."

"Take him inside. Me and Dante will finish getting the camper hooked up. We're still leaving, and after all that noise, we don't have time to fuck around out here." Damian stood naked in the middle of the lot next to his brother. I glared and snapped at Dante. What the fuck was he doing there? "He came to help when my parents called the pack on us. We'll talk about it later; no time now." Damian answered my unspoken question before picking up his pants and slipping them on.

Billy Ray tugged at my good arm until I stood. I was over a head taller than him in this form. All three of them stared at me until I started to feel a little awkward. I'd probably have some explaining to do once I figured out how to change back. I let Billy Ray lead me to the camper. After we climbed into the now cramped space, made even more so by the fact that I couldn't even stand at full height, and he found a light switch, I sat on one of the couches and let him poke and prod my arm, only grunting when he found where it was broken.

"Let me go see if I can find the first aid kit." He looked under the kitchen sink before I could get his attention and point to the little hall closet where Damian kept the kit. He nodded and grinned while going to grab it.

The door opened and Damian poked his head in. "Everything going okay in here?" Billy Ray nodded. "Okay, brace yourselves, I'm going to pull her out, and it might be a bit tough going until I get on the highway."

"I have to take care of his arm, so try not to jerk us around too much."

Damian rolled his eyes. "Yes, Mom. Just give me five minutes to get out of the park, and it shouldn't be too bad after that." He shut the door.

Billy Ray came back to me after grabbing a bottle of water out of the fridge and a towel off the counter. "I'm going to flush it out first, then put some gauze on it before I set the bone. It's going to be painful when I do that, so I want you to try to remember I'm not hurting you on purpose."

I heard the meaning behind his words—please don't hurt me for helping you even if you're in agony because of it. Giving him one nod, I braced myself for him to do what he could to fix my arm, but he was gentle at first, and I relaxed. I caught sight of myself in the darkened window and startled. The upper part of my face was almost human, but from the nose down, well, let's just say I had a snout and teeth that would give a vampire fang envy. Seeing that change made me wonder about the others. Looking down, I noticed that my body was covered in thick hair, and my hands were topped with sharp pointed nails that had blood and gunk under them. I shuddered when I saw that, and my curiosity over my state ended there.

"It's fascinating, you know." I couldn't reply or ask what he found fascinating, so I just sat there. "I mean I've never seen a werewolf in this form. Thought it was something they made up for the movies." He huffed out a laugh as he wrapped the bite mark in gauze. "You're amazing, Clay, and I think the three of us are going to do great things together."

My words came out as a bunch of gibberish because I forgot I couldn't talk, but I wanted to tell him to fuck off if he thought I was going to hang around him and Damian while they went on living their lives together. Who needed a third wheel, and what sort of sad sack would want to be one? I didn't have time to think it through too much because that's when he decided to set my arm, and then there was nothing but white-hot pain. I closed my eyes and rested my head on the window behind me.

"There. I think it's straight now, but we should probably get you to a doctor sooner rather than later." He scratched his chin. "Can you change back fully? I'm not sure you'd be welcome like that in a regular emergency room, and I don't know if any of the packs up North would be willing to have their medical staff look at you since you're, you know, what you are."

The camper jostled and bumped, making Billy Ray stumble and fall into my lap and onto my arm. I howled in pain as my arm went back to hanging at an odd angle once again.

"Ah, shit." Billy Ray scrambled out of my lap. "Sorry. I should have listened to Damian and braced myself. Going to have to do this again, and then I'll splint it quickly." He got up, ignoring my glare, to grab a couple of spoons, one wooden and the other hard plastic. Once again, he manipulated my arm, but this time he used the spoons and a dishtowel to make a brace to hold it in place before sitting down next to me. "That had to hurt, and having it done twice must have sucked."

No shit, Sherlock.

"So, about shifting, think you can?"

I shrugged. I had no idea if I could or not, and if I did, would I be left with puppy brain again? Figuring I couldn't stay half wolf, half man forever, I nodded and closed my eyes to help me focus on that feeling. My humanity was there. I just had to find it and force it to the surface. First thing I noticed was that the pain—not only in my arm—intensified. The next thing was that I was chilly as I was naked and sitting under one of the vents that was blowing cold air down on me. I shivered, because without the fur keeping me warm, it was damn cold.

"Well, guess that answers that question." Billy Ray stood. "I'll grab you something to put on." He disappeared into the bedroom, where he was going to have a hell of a time getting into the closet or drawers, because when the pop outs were closed the wall blocked half of them. His cursing made me grin, but he returned with one of Damian's ratty old T-shirts and a pair of shorts. "Couldn't get into the closet, so this will have to do."

"Thanks." I took the clothes and looked at my arm, which was throbbing in pain. "For everything."

"I should be the one thanking you. I keep thinking about what would have happened if you hadn't turned into—

whatever that was you were—to help me." He sat next to me once again and took out his phone. "I should call up to Damian and tell him you're okay and back to normal." He eyed me for a moment. "You are normal, right?"

I paused while pulling the shirt over my head to assess how my mind felt before nodding. "I think I'm fine." He grinned and then called Damian. I finished dressing while he told Damian I was fine and back in my human form, but he thought they needed to get me to a hospital to have my arm x-rayed as soon as he thought we were out of danger.

"He's not going to stop until we cross the state line, so probably Tupelo is the nearest city with a hospital. You think you can make it that long?"

"Can I take some ibuprofen or something for the pain? I feel like I got hit by a Mack truck." My face hurt as well as my neck where the rope had choked me earlier.

"You look sort of like one hit you too." He dug through the first aid kit and pulled out a little white packet containing two pills, thought about it, and snatched out the three remaining packs. Handing me the pills, he grabbed what was left of the water he'd used to rinse my arm. "Maybe you could just lie down for a bit. You should start healing up, but for your arm's sake, I hope you don't mend too fast."

Snorting, I took the pills. "Wake me up when we hit Torpedo?"

Billy Ray chuckled as he stood so I could swing my legs up onto the couch. "It's Tupelo, and yeah, if you doze off, I'll wake you up." He patted my thigh before going over to the cat crates and looking in, only to get hissed at.

"I'd leave them in there if I were you." That was the last thing I said before slipping off to sleep.

LOUD VOICES WOKE me. Rubbing my face, I turned to see what the commotion was about. Damian, Billy Ray, and Dante were standing in the cramped kitchen area, and apparently Billy Ray wasn't too happy about something.

"You're the reason we're in this mess." Billy Ray spat the words in Dante's face before turning to Damian. "It was all his idea, taking Clay, using the app to get him, all him."

"Just calm down." Damian's head swiveled between the two men. "He's explained some stuff to me, and I think if you'd just listen, and maybe remember that he showed up to help when he knew what was happening, you'd see it's not all his fault."

"I'm sorry for making you a part of—"

"It was your plan!" Billy Ray raised his voice to cut Dante off as if that would get his point across.

"I was fucked up. Your scent was clouding my judgement. I never would have betrayed my brother if I hadn't been high on you." Dante's lips twisted. "It's disgusting to think I fucking wanted you like that."

"I'm perfectly aware of your feelings for me."

"Okay, just shut up, both of you." Damian stepped between them, and that's when I noticed the bruises on his face and neck, although they were already fading, as were the scratches on his arms.

"Why don't all three of you shut the fuck up? You're giving me an even bigger headache, and that's saying something, considering the way my head's already pounding." I sat up and glared at them.

Damian rushed across the room to sit on the couch and pull me into his arms. "Fuck, I was so scared you were going to be fucked up again after shifting not once, but twice."

I wriggled to get out of his grasp, but he held on and didn't let me go. "I'm fine. Well, except for the aching head and throbbing in my broken arm." Finally, I relaxed and let him hug me, figuring there was no point in fighting him. "Where are we?"

"At a park outside Tupelo." Damian pulled back enough to look at my face. "Billy Ray said you needed to go to the emergency room, and I thought it would be too late to get back on the road after that if the emergency room here is like every other one I've ever been to."

"We'll spend the night here, and then we can drive straight through tomorrow." Billy Ray came to join us but sent a warning look in Dante's direction, when he tried to follow, which stopped him in his tracks. He sat on the side opposite Damian and put his arm around my shoulders. "I know I said this already, but thanks again for protecting me." He squeezed me tighter than Damian had, and I sighed.

"Okay, you want to take my truck to the hospital?" Dante looked uncomfortable as he watched the over-the-top displays of affection.

"You drove your own truck?" Don't ask me why that was the question my mind came up with, instead of asking why the fuck he was there in the first place.

"I figured I'd need transportation." He shrugged and looked down at his feet.

"He's coming with us?" I asked Damian, who'd let me go and sat back to watch all of us.

"I can't send him back. JR knows he was there and fighting on the wrong side."

"I think it's a stupid idea to take him. What if he's a spy for the pack or even just for your parents?" Billy Ray wasn't properly hugging me any longer; only one arm was around my back while the other hand rested on my thigh in an almost possessive gesture.

"We'll take him with us." Damian made eye contact with Billy Ray first, then me, as if he was gauging how big of a fight he was going to have against bringing his brother along. When neither of us put up a fuss, he turned to Dante. "I'm taking you with us to Minnesota, but once we get there, you're on your own when it comes to the pack. I'm not pulling any strings to get you accepted."

"Wait. We're going back to the Outcast pack?" I couldn't believe he'd want to go somewhere we were less safe than with his parents; at least they only wanted to kill one of us.

"We'll talk about it after you get that arm looked at." Damian got up and disappeared into the bedroom, only to return with some of my clothes, ones I hardly ever wore, which was when I remembered all my stuff was back at the motel. Well, I guessed losing my computer was a small price to pay for getting out of Alabama alive. Fuck Alabama.

Chapter Fourteen

DAMIAN

After deciding that I'd accompany Clay to the emergency room, he and I left Dante and Billy Ray to set up the camper for the night—only after I threatened Dante's life if he dared to touch Billy Ray. I'm not sure if it was my threat or the look on Clay's face and the memory of what he could change into at a whim that made Dante agree and almost cower away when I brought it up, but I didn't care as long as he kept his hands off my mate. It was already after midnight when we began our long, uncomfortable, silent drive to the hospital and was approaching four in the morning by the time we got back. Billy Ray met us at the door.

"He's fine, but we had to tell the doctor he'd broken it a couple of weeks ago. God, I hate going to a regular hospital for shit like this." We healed too fast for human medicine, and Clay's Xray made the doctor question our explanation of when it had happened. He'd also not been impressed with how it was healing and watching them rebreak the arm had made my stomach twist into a knot. At least they'd given him some pain relief beforehand, unfortunately not enough for a werewolf's metabolism. Clay felt most of it but had to pretend he didn't, so as not to raise any questions. Reaching out, I offered a hand to Clay, who knocked it away with his good arm and brushed past Billy Ray without a word.

"I see he's still pissed at me." Billy Ray's lips twisted into a grimace while he watched Clay walk to the bedroom.

"He's pissed at both of us, and I can't really blame him." He had a right to be angry at me, but I hoped to make him understand. If I was going to do that, I'd need Billy Ray to give us some space. "How was Dante after we left?"

Shrugging, Billy Ray followed me into the kitchen area from where we could see Dante on one of the convertible couches, sleeping between my cats, who'd been more than a little miffed at me when I'd released them from their cages after we'd stopped. He was snoring and oblivious to the world, which reminded me of when we were kids and he slept through a tornado even after my dad had carried him down to the cellar.

"He kept his distance and then fell asleep right after we were done hooking up the camper." He stepped in close to me, and instinctively, I put my arms around him. "I'll sleep on the other couch."

Pulling away, I looked into his eyes to try to get a handle on how he was feeling. "Are you sure? Because I was thinking it might work better if I could have a little time alone with Clay to see if I can make him understand. I didn't know how to ask you to sleep on the couch, though."

"I understand, and I'm fine with it. I know you have feelings for Clay that run deeper than the ones you have for me. I'm just your bonded mate; doesn't mean you love me." Billy Ray pulled free of my arms and turned away.

I put my hand on his shoulder, unable to find the words to comfort him because it was true. I loved Clay, and while I felt something for Billy Ray, it wasn't love. The feelings were spurred by the bond, not my heart, and I wasn't sure I liked it. It gave me a new appreciation for how Clay felt when his beast insisted on being with me. "I'm sorry." Pathetic I know, but what else was there to say.

His eyes sparkled when he turned back. "Don't be. I knew what I was getting into when we consummated the bond. I just didn't think it would be too hard to convince someone that having two hot men in his bed was better than one, but it looks like Clay's going to be just as stubborn about this as everything else." He grinned, but it was pained, and my quiet chuckle was forced.

"Let me go talk to him. If he'll even let me in the room with him, that is." After giving Billy Ray a peck on the cheek, I left him to make his bed while I went to face the music alone.

After knocking and getting no response, I slowly opened the door to find Clay lying on the bed. He was only wearing a pair of boxer briefs and the cast, which we could probably remove in less than a week because he'd be completely healed by then. "Hey." I'll admit it wasn't the cleverest thing I could say, but again I was at a loss for words.

He rolled his head to look at me. "Thought you'd be keeping Billy Ray company tonight." Shifting to look at the ceiling once again, the set of his jaw told me he was holding back all the stuff he wanted to say.

"We need to talk." It was that simple. We needed to hash this all out before it drove an immovable wedge between us—if it hadn't already.

"I'm not sure there's anything to talk about. You fucked Billy Ray. You've made your choice, and it obviously wasn't me."

"You're the one who kept me at arm's length because you didn't think anything you felt for me could be real because of your beast. You're the one still holding a grudge against me for something you did to yourself. Tell me what you'd do if you were me." Having to point those things out to Clay wasn't my favorite thing to do. It felt like I was trying to justify cheating on him, but it was all true. He'd made me feel like I could never make it right between us because I'd infected him, and no matter how I tried, I couldn't make him love me, or even like me, for that matter.

"So, basically you're saying that you cheating on me is my fault. Got it, now go away."

Sighing, I closed the door and leaned against it. I wasn't leaving until we'd resolved everything. "That's not what I meant, and you know it, just like you know what I said is true. I'm not sure what I can do to make you see how I feel about you. I'd have thought that seeing I'd fulfilled the mate bond with Billy Ray and still wanted you more than him, would have been enough, but I guess I was wrong."

The muscle in his jaw twitched, but he said nothing.

"I'm not in love with Billy Ray, not the way I am with you." The truth hurt, but maybe if he actually heard the words said out loud, he'd believe them. I didn't expect his reaction and had no time to prepare when he jumped off the bed and pinned me to the door. The hard plaster of his cast pressed against the underside of my chin when he put his arm across my neck.

"If you loved me, you wouldn't have fucked him." He snarled into my face, and I wondered how much control he had over his newfound powers to change into the wolfman. Would he shift and kill me if he got angry enough?

"It's not like that. I can't explain the biology behind it, but I was compelled to do it. I know it's not an excuse, but when I thought you'd slept with him, I was just so jealous I forgot about keeping my distance from him. I couldn't control what nature put in motion, but knowing what I know now, I'm not sure I would change anything." I choked when he pressed harder on my neck, cutting off my air.

"You'd cheat on me again? Good to know."

Shaking my head wasn't the best way to get my reaction to that across, but I couldn't speak so it had to do.

"I can't believe I thought I had feelings for someone like you. This is why I only do hookups." He jerked away from me so quickly that I fell to my knees, clutching my neck and gasping for breath as I did. He dropped down onto the bed and put his head in his hands. "I don't need this shit. I don't want this shit. Why can't my life just go back to the way it was?"

Once I was breathing normally again, I got to my knees and shuffled over to him. He didn't look at me or try to push me away when I put my hands by his elbows on his knees. "I'm sorry, but I can't keep feeling guilty for you getting infected because I can't change it, even if I wanted to. It doesn't do either one of us any good to wish it was different, and me shouldering all the responsibility for something I was only partially to blame for isn't helping. I want to make a life with you but not based on the feeling that I have to because I'm the one who fucked up your life."

"I don't know if I can get past this."

I wasn't sure which of the things he was talking about. The infection or me sleeping with Billy Ray? Which one couldn't he move beyond, and did it matter? It did because if he couldn't forgive me, there was no future for us. "Can you try?"

He snorted. "Try?"

"Tell me what I can do to help you try to get past it." Still not knowing which it was, I was more than willing to do anything if it meant keeping Clay in my life.

"Throw Billy Ray out?" It sounded more like a question than a statement that made me wonder if he really meant it.

"Would that make you happy?"

He shook his head. "I don't know." He finally looked at me. "No, after seeing what he has to look forward to if he doesn't have you to protect him, no, it wouldn't make me happy. Even if I hate him more than anything in the world right now, I wouldn't want to see him with someone like JR."

"It wasn't just me there protecting him; you did most of it. If you hadn't been there…" I shuddered at the thought, but it brought up one of the points Billy Ray wanted me to make to plead our case to Clay. "Billy Ray did some research on the mate bond, and it's not uncommon for a mated pair to have a third."

Clay cocked a brow at me, and I almost smiled because he looked like the old Clay for a minute. "Are you trying to lure me into some kind of kinky threesome thing?"

"Is it working?" I shrugged like it was some off-handed comment, but really, I hoped it would work. I knew Clay liked sex—just like most other red-blooded man—so offering him two men in his bed couldn't be a bad thing, could it?

"No, not really."

Shit. That wasn't the response I'd hoped for. "What can I do then?"

"I don't know. I think I need some time to think things over." Clay stood, making my hands fall from his knees. He went around the bed, pulled down the sheet, and crawled in.

Standing, I felt defeated. "I'll leave you to do that then." I went to the door, but just before I could open it, his voice stopped me.

"You can sleep in here if you want. Those couches aren't that comfortable, and I assume you'll have to drive most of the day tomorrow, so you should get a good night's sleep."

My heart rate ticked up a notch. Was this his way of telling me he might forgive me? "Yeah, well a good night's sleep is probably not going to happen in the four hours we have until I want to head out, but I'll take what I can get." I slipped out of my shoes, then pants and shirt, before crawling into bed with him. He lay with his back to me on the farthest edge of the bed, and I took that to mean I should stay away. That didn't mean I couldn't stare at the back of his head until I fell asleep, which turned out to be only a minute or so after I lay down.

IT TOOK SOME time for us to figure out who was riding with who. In the end, Dante ended up driving solo while I had both Billy Ray and Clay in my truck with me. We all had a travel mug of coffee, and I'd made sure to program the route into Dante's GPS so if we got separated on the road he'd still know where to go. We'd stop in St Louis, and then Clay would take over driving for Dante while Billy Ray would drive my truck to Iowa City where we'd spend the night if we didn't feel like driving straight through. I was pushing for going the distance, since I was sure I could nap while Billy Ray drove, but I wasn't sure about Dante.

The drive started out quiet as both my passengers concentrated on anything but each other. Clay was in the front while Billy Ray sat in the back. I ignored the tension in the truck, glad that I had an excuse in driving. It was almost two hours into the drive when Clay sighed loudly and turned in his seat so he could see both me and Billy Ray.

"I hate you both."

"Nice." Billy Ray sounded about as thrilled with Clay's declaration as I felt.

"I don't know how to stop hating you, or even if I want to." Clay shifted so he was looking more at Billy Ray. "But until we know what's going to happen, I can't leave you two to fend for yourselves. Even with Damian's little brother to help, you guys need someone to protect you, and I guess I'm that someone for now."

Looking in the rearview mirror, I caught the slight uptick of Billy Ray's lips before he realized that smiling at a time like this was not a good idea and schooled his expression. "That's very considerate of you, and we accept your offer."

"So, he's your spokesman now?" Clay looked at me, pursing his lips as he did.

"No, but I'm not the one who needs the extra protection, so I'll let him speak for me this time. I'm happy to have you by my side and hope you'll eventually see past your hate." Taking my eyes off the road for a moment, I made eye contact with the expectation that he'd see how much I wanted him to stop hating me.

"Well, once we get to the pack, and you guys get situated, I don't see any reason for me to hang around. I'll make sure no one there is going to fuck with you, and then I'll figure out what I'm going to do." He turned back to face forward.

"You don't want to be a lone wolf. You should stay with the pack, even if you don't want to be with us." I couldn't help it. I didn't want him out on his own. I wanted him close where I could still see him, even if it was just from afar.

"Us." Clay muttered the word and shook his head before looking out the window to hide his expression from me. "Like I said, I'll figure it out when I know what's up with the two of you."

Billy Ray and I locked eyes in the mirror. I wondered if he was thinking what I was thinking. If Clay cared enough about us to want to make sure we were safe, maybe he didn't hate us as much as he said he did.

Chapter Fifteen

BILLY RAY

After stopping for gas and lunch, Damian went to the camper to sleep. Since no one thought having Dante in a vehicle with either me or Clay was a good idea, he joined his brother in the trailer. I was fine with being left alone to drive Damian's truck. It gave me time to decompress. Spending time with Clay and Damian had seriously worn me down, and it was nice to crank up the radio and sing at the top of my lungs. Iowa City came up too fast. When we pulled over at the rest stop just outside of town, I wasn't ready to be with people again but got out of the truck any way.

"Hey." I greeted Clay, who looked like shit when he crawled out from behind the wheel of Dante's pickup. He nodded, then stretched a little as he watched the camper door. "I'll go tell them we're here and see what Damian wants to do." Another nod from Clay—he sure was talkative. Before I could get to the door, it popped open, and Dante walked out followed by a yawning Damian.

"That was quick. Did you two speed?" Damian grinned as he joked with us, but it fell flat because Clay turned away to look out over the corn field.

"Did you get enough sleep?" I hoped he'd say yes because I wanted to keep going to avoid another awkward night in the camper.

"I think so. How about you, little brother? Feel like you can drive some more?"

Dante had been watching Clay, but he snapped his attention back to Damian. "Uh, yeah, I think so. I mean, we can always switch up later, right?"

"I was thinking if you two go nap in the camper, we should be able to work out a driving schedule to make it back tonight without any of us falling asleep at the wheel." Damian looked to Clay who was still ignoring us. "What do you think, Clay?"

Clay shrugged as he turned around. "I guess that makes sense."

"Then let's get rolling again, unless anyone wants to stop somewhere to eat." Damian looked anxious to get going again.

"I'm good. I can just make a sandwich." I didn't want to hold him up because I was feeling a bit peckish.

"You can make me one, too, and I'll be good." Clay opened the door to the camper and went in.

"Guess I'm making sandwiches. You two want one?"

"No, I grabbed something while he was sleeping." Dante got in his truck and fiddled with the GPS.

"I'm good. I ate a bowl of cereal before I fell asleep. Are you sure you'll be all right in there with Clay?" Damian's brow crinkled as he thought. "Maybe you should sleep in the back seat instead."

"No, I'll be fine. If he's as tired as I am, we won't have time to do anything but gobble down a sandwich and then drop dead of exhaustion." I tried to smile to reassure him that I was fine, but he didn't seem to be buying it. "Really, what's he going to do to me?"

"You did see that thing he turned into, right?"

I laughed, making him frown, but it was too funny. "He was still himself in that form. He knew what he was doing. Even when I set his arm, which is hella painful, he didn't react without thinking about it first."

"If you're sure, then—"

"Hey, Damian, you might want to see this." Dante interrupted and shoved his phone in Damian's face. "He's fucking dead. You know what that means, right?"

Damian nodded. "Yep, I do. It means we need to haul ass and get us some protection from the pack back home."

"They won't let this slide. You know the Luptons. They'll want blood for this." Dante's eyes were wide with fright.

"They can't do anything. Clay was protecting me and Damian. JR was trying to rape me and kill Damian. Both those things break pack rules and exonerate Clay." Not that I'd believe my own words. I knew the Luptons, and just as Dante said, they'd demand blood in exchange for their loss.

"Let's get the hell out of here. The more miles we put between us and them the better."

"We'll never be able to run far enough, and if your pack finds out what we're running from, how likely are they to want us?" Dante shoved his phone back in his pocket. "And what about Mom and Dad?"

"What about them?" Damian looked ready for a fight at just the mention of his parents.

"They'll be in danger."

"I don't care, or did you forget they kidnapped Clay and were going to kill him? Oh, wait, I forgot, you were there helping them." Damian backed Dante up so he was leaning against his truck. "You want to turn around and go back to help them, be my guest, but my first priority is getting me and mine somewhere safe."

"Damian." I grabbed his arm. "Dante is right about your parents being in trouble if they stay. Maybe he should call them and see if they need—"

"No. He either chooses us or them. There's no fence-sitting on this one."

Dante's angry glare softened just a little. "Okay, I understand. You're taking a huge leap in trusting me after what I did. I'm going with you. It's time for Mom and Dad to own up to the things they did. JR wouldn't be dead right now if they hadn't called the Luptons and ratted you out."

Damian's shoulders relaxed, and he pulled Dante into a hug. "I'm sorry to make you choose, but I just can't with them anymore."

"I get it. I really do." Dante clapped his brother on the back before pulling away. "I missed you too much to lose you again. Plus, I'm scared shitless to go back there." His lopsided grin made both me and Damian smile.

"You guys going to stand around hugging all day, or what?" Clay sounded impatient when he stuck his head out the door to ask his question.

Looking over his shoulder at Clay, Damian answered him. "We're getting ready to roll, in a sec." Clay grunted and slammed the door.

"Are you going to tell him?" I wondered how Clay would take the news that he'd killed someone.

"Not right now. He'll probably freak out, and I'd much rather have some backup when he does. Him and Pete are pretty close, maybe I'll have him help me break the news to Clay. Now, let's get out of here. Be careful in there, and if he causes you any trouble just send me a text, and I'll pull over." He leaned in and brushed his lips across my cheek. I wanted more but took what I could get, knowing that any sort of affection he showed me was better than nothing.

"I'm sure I'll be fine." I nodded at Dante who'd climbed back into his truck and gave me a little wave while mouthing "Good luck."

Once in the camper, I went straight to the kitchen to make the sandwiches, wondering why Clay hadn't done it while he was waiting. I slapped some mayo on bread and then turkey and lettuce. I'd just cut them in half when the trailer jerked, making me brace myself on the counter until it steadied when Damian hit cruising speed. Then I put the sandwiches on two paper plates and grabbed a bag of chips from the cupboard.

"Food's done." I raised my voice since Clay was in the bedroom, and he came out looking like he'd already been asleep. He snatched one of the plates and the bag of chips off the counter and carried them into the living room to sit on the couch where I'd planned on sleeping. I stood and ate my food while watching him devour his.

"I'm not going to jump you so you can stop staring at me."

"I wasn't staring at you because of that." I finished my food, threw the plate into the recycling bin, and grabbed a water out of the fridge. "You want one?"

"Sure." Clay shoved more chips in his mouth and then asked, "So why *were* you watching me then?"

Shrugging, I handed him a bottle of water and sat down on the other end of the couch. One of the big cats lifted its head from the chair it was laying on and gave me a death glare before going back to its nap. "Those cats give me the heebie-jeebies."

"Well, they don't care much for you either." He grunted and tore off a tiny piece of his sandwich that he then held down by his ankles while he made kissy noises. The monster-sized feline was there in a second to take the offered food and then slinked its way around Clay's ankles. "They love me, though."

His tone made me wonder if that was a pointed barb at me about how Damian felt about the two of us. I knew he loved Clay and me, well, not so much, but did Clay really need to rub it in? "I'm sure it's because you've spent more time with them. They'll learn to love me because I'm a loveable sort of guy."

Clay choked on the food in his mouth and started coughing so hard I thought he might keel over and die. When he was finally able to breathe again, he looked at me with watery eyes. "You have a high opinion of yourself, don't you?"

"Not really, but I can hope." I stood and grabbed one of the blankets that were stored above the couch in a cabinet. "You're on my bed."

"Yeah, I guess I am." He stood and brushed the potato chip crumbs off his legs. "You know the Outcast pack is just as fucked up as yours, right?"

"Damian mentioned they'd had some problems, but he said the alpha called him to explain that they'd taken care of it and you and he were welcome to come back." I spread my blanket out and sat down.

"Their alpha is like me."

Cocking my head, I looked up at him, trying to see what he was saying without actually saying. "Infected, you mean, right?" He nodded. "That's cool. I have no problems with non-genetic weres. That wasn't something I was raised with. My pack had rules against knowingly infecting humans, but if one got accidentally infected, we did our best to integrate them." I wasn't going to tell him one of our rules called for sterilization to get accepted, but I viewed that as much less harsh than death.

"Well, that's good to hear. I'm going to go get some sleep."

"Good night."

He waved at me over his shoulder before disappearing into the bedroom, leaving me to wonder what he'd really wanted to say. Maybe he was looking for acceptance? I couldn't know how it was to be suddenly thrust into this world. Hell, it was hard enough navigating through it when you were born into it. I rolled over and shut my eyes. Sleep came quickly, even with my mind running a mile a minute.

"TURN HERE AND pull off to the side of the road."

I did as Damian instructed and parked the rig in front of a double-wide trailer that had a huge garage and another structure attached to it. Even though it was almost 1:30 in the morning, there were lights shining from the windows and silhouettes of people moving around inside.

"Aww, they waited up for us. How sweet." Clay leaned forward to rest his chin on the back of the seat. "They probably have a hard-on for the two of you, huh?"

"What the hell are you talking about?" Damian turned to glare at Clay who'd been trying to push our buttons since he'd switched out with Dante after the Twin Cities, claiming his arm was too sore for him to drive anymore.

"A mated pair is quite the coup for a pack of misfits like them."

"Shut up." Damian opened his door and got out just as Dante came from where he'd parked his truck behind us.

"Don't know why he's so touchy. They almost got him killed twice, you'd think he'd have learned his lesson, but, oh well, third time's the charm, right?" Clay said, grinning at me before sliding over and getting out.

I joined them on the walk up to the front door, but before we got up the steps a man opened the door and stepped out. His smile appeared to be genuine as he pulled Damian into a bear hug that lifted him off his feet. "I'm so glad you decided to come home," he said as he released Damian, only to do the same to Clay, who struggled, making the big man chuckle. "Good to see you too, Clay." He turned to me, and I stepped back behind Damian. "You must be Billy Ray." He held out his hand to me, and I took it. "Heard a lot about you, young man, it's nice to finally meet you."

"And you, sir." I was nervous all of a sudden. It felt like I was there for a job interview and every word out of my mouth either counted for or against me.

"No sirs around here; call me Willard." I nodded, and he turned to Dante. "Dante, I presume." They shook hands as I followed Clay and Damian into the house where they received more hugs from another man who could only be Pete, and behind him stood a thin woman who was crying silently into a handkerchief.

"Billy Ray, this is Pete and Minnie." Damian introduced me and went to hug the woman, who was clinging to Clay like he'd disappear if she let go of him.

"Nice to meet you, Pete." I offered my hand, but he didn't take it. I wondered if I'd offended him by using his name and not a formal title since he was the alpha. "I mean, sir." I shifted nervously, and just as I was going to take my hand back, he took it.

He grinned, and then pulled me into a hug that was nowhere near as violent as those his partner had been doling out on the porch. "Call me Pete. We're not formal around these parts."

"Okay, Pete it is." I'd barely gotten out of Pete's grasp when the lady, Minnie, pulled me to her with boney arms that were much stronger than they appeared. "And you're Minnie, right?" I wanted to make sure I got the names right.

"I am, and I'm just as pleased to have you here as I am to have those two boys back where they belong." She kissed my cheek before releasing me. "How about some refreshments?" She didn't wait for an answer before hustling off; I assumed to get the refreshments no one had said they wanted.

We gathered in the living room, which gave off a homey, lived-in vibe. Me, Damian, and Clay sat on the couch while the two older men took the recliners across from us, leaving Dante to sit off to the side on a not so comfortable-looking arm chair. Minnie didn't sit after she delivered a platter of cheese and crackers and glasses with a bottle of whiskey; instead, she hovered like a hummingbird. I swore I heard a sound coming off her like vibrating strings on a plucked guitar and wondered if she was always this anxious or if she suspected something was going to happen.

"So, you've brought an extra or two with you. Want to tell us what's going on?" Pete filled the glasses as he asked, like he wasn't dying to know why we all turned up on his doorstep in the middle of the night.

"I told you we needed to get out of Alabama." Damian accepted the glass and threw back the liquid before holding it out again. Pete chuckled and refilled the glass before he finished pouring the first round for the rest of us.

"That you did, but I think we need some more information just in case we get a call from the central council." He filled his glass last and sat back waiting for his answer.

"It's my fault we had to run." Clay's voice was barely audible over the rustle of people raising glasses and taking snacks from the platter. All eyes turned to him. "They found out I was infected. They wanted Damian to agree to stay, and then they attacked us. I think I might have killed at least one of them."

Everyone's mouth dropped open in surprise. The three elders because they hadn't heard all the details, and the three of us because we had no idea Clay might have known what he'd done to JR.

"Well, I guess it's going to be a long night then."

Understatement of the year there, Willard.

Chapter Sixteen

CLAY

It was late, but that didn't stop Pete from taking me into the backroom that held an office of sorts to have a private chat, while Willard and Minnie found places for all of us to sleep. Damian argued that we could sleep in the camper, but they weren't having it. There was no electricity or water at Damian's house. Since he'd left, they'd disconnected everything, but it stood empty because they were hoping he'd return. I kind of wanted to go home, but knew I couldn't make the drive back to the house in Grebes, which I'd inherited from my parents, in the shape I was in—falling asleep at the wheel wouldn't do any of us any good.

Pete sat in the desk chair, and I took the other one facing him. After pulling out another bottle of whiskey, he sat back and studied me, making me fidget until he decided it was time to speak. "So, you managed to control the change. Congratulations, that's the biggest hurdle most of us face."

"I did, but I think I may have scared the crap out of Damian and Billy Ray." The way I said Billy Ray's name made Pete frown. "I mean, they didn't know I could do that. I never told Damian the stuff you told me I should be able to do that the genetic wolves can't do."

Pete nodded and filled us both a glass. "Yeah, it's better to play your cards close to the vest, but I think with Damian you're safe. From the way it sounds, he's planning on staying with you for the long haul."

I snorted and ended up burning my nostrils because I'd just taken a drink. "I doubt that. He's got Billy Ray now."

"You're one stubborn asshole, aren't you?" Pete put his glass on the desk, his elbows followed so he could lean forward. "He's got it so bad for you. I don't know how you can't see that."

"Maybe because he fucked another man?"

"Fucking has nothing to do with love. I thought you knew that, given the way you met Damian." He raised his eyebrows.

"Okay, fine, but we were living together, and he fucked Billy Ray. What I want to know is this; did he have a choice? Like, this mate bond thing, was it something that was going to happen no matter what? Or could he have said no and left?" It had been bugging me since that night in the hotel. I was hoping Pete would tell me that Damian had no choice in the matter because then, maybe, I could see past what he'd done.

"He had a choice." Pete held up his hand to shut me up. Pursing my lips, I bit back all the nasty things I had to say about Damian. "But...there's biology behind the bond. If he was in close proximity to his mate, his body would respond to Billy Ray's pheromones. The urge to complete the bond would have been overwhelming. That being said, he could have resisted."

"Can I call him a bastard now?" Hearing Pete tell me that Damian didn't have to fuck Billy Ray, that he'd wanted to, made me so angry I could spit.

"You can, but maybe you need to step back and look at the whole picture."

"What whole picture? All I can see is red because if you'd asked me which one of us was more likely to cheat, I would have said me."

"Did he really cheat on you? Did you tell him that you considered your relationship to be monogamous?"

No, dammit, I hadn't. If anything, I'd tried to make it seem like we weren't even together more than for convenience and to get off. Was this my fault?

"I can see your answer on your face."

"Yeah, I fucking know, but still, I didn't fuck Billy Ray. He thought I did, and he was pissed then."

Pete shook his head. "You are one stubborn asshole."

"So you said before." I gulped what was left of my whiskey and let him refill the glass.

"Damian loves you, and I'm sure you know that. He was angry and probably went there to beat the hell out of Billy Ray, because I know him, and that's how he'd think. He couldn't beat you up because he loves you, so he'd take it out on the other party."

Fuck, that sounded exactly like Damian. "What do I do now? I can see how he looks at Billy Ray, and it's different than before. Where do I fit in?"

"Do you love Damian?"

Wow, Pete really knew how to get straight to the heart of the matter. Did I love Damian? Hell yes, I did. I'd realized it too late to do anything about it, but I did. "I do."

"Okay, that's a start. The next step is telling him that."

I shook my head so hard that I popped a muscle and had to stop to rub the ache away. "No way."

"Yes, way, and then you three need to sit down and talk. I have a feeling Billy Ray might have some ideas that will surprise you."

"Oh, like me fucking off and dying?" It's what I wanted Billy Ray to do. Why should I think he felt differently about me? *Because you know, he told you and so did Damian. You just didn't want to hear it.*

"I'm not going to say you're a stubborn asshole again because that's getting a bit overused, but if the shoe fits..." Pete shrugged and sat back in the chair, putting his hands behind his head. He looked up at the ceiling. "I think it's time to share with you a little bit about my own relationship."

"I really don't need to hear your epic love story right now." Last thing I needed was to hear about someone else's happy ever after when my own had just disappeared.

"Ha! If only." He trained his eyes on me, pinning me to the chair with his intensity. "You think just because Willard loved me enough to defy the laws of his pack to infect me that everything was easy for us? That we didn't have to go through tons of shit to get where we are today?"

"No, I suppose you having to start your own pack tipped me off that everything wasn't that easy."

"Oh, that's not the half of it. You need to learn about werewolves and what being one entails. There's more to it than shifting into your other form during the full moon. There are power dynamics that mean life or death, not only for those of us in charge, but also for those we protect. Do you think being a pack leader or elder is just some fancy title and presiding over the monthly meetings?" He paused, and I thought he wanted a response from me, but then he answered his own question. "No, it's about keeping our people safe, the lowest of the low, the ones who can't protect themselves. Keeping our secret is our top priority because that's what keeps us safest, but there are so many other things we have to deal with. You have no idea, but I think you will soon."

"Okay I get it. I get it." Not all of it, because why would I soon know what it meant to be in charge of a pack?

"Okay so here's the thing. Willard has a bonded mate." He paused for dramatic effect which he'd more than achieved because my mind was blown.

"Who?"

"Minnie."

"No way!" I had no idea that Willard was bisexual, let alone that he had someone on the side.

"Yes, way. So, you see, I know what you're going through because I've been there."

"But, Minnie and Willard?"

Pete nodded. "And me."

"Wait. So you're saying you three…" I couldn't wrap my mind around what he was telling me.

"Well, not in the way you're probably imagining it. Minnie is on the asexual spectrum, and Willard and I are gay, so there's little more than cuddling that goes on between her and us." He grinned as he watched me try to puzzle it out. "She and Willard agreed that after the bond was completed they really didn't want anything more to do with each other sexually. Minnie had been worried that her mate would be disappointed in her lack of interest in the physical side of a relationship, while at the same time Willard had always worried that his mate would be repulsed by the fact that he's a man, if his mate turned out to be a man, or that he was gay, if it was a woman. That happens sometimes, you know. A heterosexual man will find out his mate is a man, and then things can get ugly. More than one gay man has been killed when their mate found them."

"So Mother Nature doesn't always know best then?"

He chuckled. "She does like to throw a curve ball out there occasionally. But in this case, it worked out for everyone involved."

"I still don't see what any of that has to do with me."

"Really? You don't see any sort of parallel here? Like at all?" Pete stared at me like I should know the answer to this, and I was just being dense.

Then what he was saying hit me, and I rolled my eyes. "But it's not the same. You said yourself both Minnie and Willard were relieved that they didn't have to be together. Damian and Billy Ray are nothing like that."

"I know it's not the exact same situation, but there's more than just who's sleeping in whose bed here. This is where the power dynamic comes in. They need you. And though I don't believe in destiny or that there's a path set out for us by some higher being, I do think you are right where you were intended to be, with the ones who need you most." Pete sighed. "I can't tell you what to do, but if you love Damian like you say you do, you'll try to figure out how to make things work, with not only him, but with Billy Ray too."

"I doubt there's a way to do that."

"There is if you're willing. There's more than one way to have a relationship, and contrary to what everyone likes to think, people can love more than one person. The capacity to love is not limited. And though this might sound funny when you've been around people who have the mate bond, the one true love bullshit is just that, bullshit." After laying that heavy bit of wisdom on me, he looked at his watch and yawned. "I think we should call it a night. You sleep on what I said, and if you need, we can talk more tomorrow after we get Damian back in his house."

I stood and followed him out into the living room where Dante was fast asleep on the couch, the cats once again sleeping with him. Traitors. I hated those damn cats and their fickle affections. There was a cot set up in the corner where Billy Ray lay. He wasn't sleeping but looked like he could drop off at any minute. He smiled at me when he noticed me looking at him, so I quickly turned away.

"Where's Damian, and where am I supposed to sleep?"

"The answer to both your questions is down the hall, first door on the right." Pete patted my shoulder as he passed. "Good night boys."

"Night, Pete." Billy Ray and I said it at the same time, making me wince.

I didn't bother telling him good night; instead, I walked down the hallway like a man heading to the electric chair. Why did they think it was a good idea to put the two of us in the same room? Oh, because it was Pete and Willard, that's why.

Damian looked like he was sleeping when I silently crept into the room. It was the same bed he'd recovered in when Blaine had attacked me only a few months before. The thought brought back memories I'd rather forget because they tangled with more recent ones that involved the feeling of holding a limp body in my hands, and not caring that I might have killed a man to protect what was mine.

Damian didn't move as I stripped down to my underwear and crawled under the covers, leaving half the bed between us. "I told Willard that he should have set up another cot, but he said they only had the one." His voice startled me.

"I figured it was his doing." If we didn't work things out, they'd probably lock us in a closet next. "I had an interesting chat with Pete."

Rolling over to face me, Damian looked wide awake. "Oh, what did you two talk about, or is it secret infected werewolf stuff?" The corner of his lip lifted to let me know he was attempting a joke.

"Did you know about Minnie?"

"I know lots of things about Minnie. She's a great lady." Was he deflecting because he didn't want to spill their secret?

"Okay, did you know that Minnie is Willard's bonded mate?"

Damian popped up into a sitting position. "Oh my god!"

"Sh, not so loud. People are sleeping." I wanted to laugh at his reaction but shut it down before the sound made it out of my mouth.

He lay back on his side, head resting on his hand so he was looking down at me. "You have to tell me the whole story because this has got to be good."

"You sound like an old church lady wanting all the hot gossip."

He reached out and hesitated just a moment before pushing my shoulder. "Come on, this is the strangest news I've ever heard. You can't hold out on me." His grin turned into a full-fledged smile, and my stomach flip-flopped. It had been days since I'd seen him smile, and I hadn't realized how much I missed it.

"Fine, the condensed version because I'm too damn tired to talk much more. Willard and Minnie are bonded mates. Willard is gay. Minnie's asexual. They made a deal to complete the bond but keep it secret while Willard infected Pete so they could be together. They're all in a weird sort of threesome because of power, or some shit that I don't completely get." I yawned because I really was tired.

"I know why he told you his story then." The smile slipped from his lips as they pursed, and the expression on his face hardened. "They just can't help meddling."

"It seems to be their purpose in life." I shrugged because what could I do about it?

"You understand what Pete telling you all that was meant to accomplish, right?"

"I'm assuming he was hoping I'd see that even though I'm mad as hell at you right now, there's a way to move forward without one of us having to give up something they want."

Damian's brow furrowed as he studied me in the light coming from the window. The full moon phase was only a few days away so there was plenty of light. "What is it that you want?"

It was the moment of truth, and I wasn't sure I could do it. Turning away so I didn't have to look at him when I said it, I took a deep breath. "I want you." There I'd admitted it, even if it hurt. I didn't fight him when he pulled me into his arms. I was done fighting, but I wanted to make one thing clear to him. "I'm not thrilled with what you did, but I see the part I played in it too. Not that it excuses anything, or that I think I'm the reason you cheated, or that I deserved for you to do it, but I get that I should have told you sooner how I felt. I should have made it clear that I thought we weren't fucking other people anymore."

He buried his face in my neck, his breath sending shivers down my spine and raising gooseflesh on my arms. "I fucked up, and I take full responsibility for it. I can apologize for hurting you, but I'm not sorry it happened. I need Billy Ray. You can't ever know how it feels to have that missing piece put into place. I'm so much stronger now. I know I can handle the shit that comes our way, because there's always shit, and with you next to me, nothing will stop us."

It hurt me deeply to hear that he needed Billy Ray, but I knew on some level he had little choice in the matter now that he'd completed the bond. "I don't like Billy Ray. I'll share you with him because I have no other choice, but I'd appreciate it if you could not rub it in my face too much." Watching the man I loved love another man on the side was not how I'd thought I'd end up living my life, but it was the only choice I had if I wanted to keep Damian.

He pulled his face out of my neck and brushed his lips across mine. "I don't love him either. It's you I want, has been since I first laid eyes on you."

"That was just lust." I snorted and rolled my eyes.

"How do you think most relationships start, sweetheart?"

Grimacing at his use of a term of endearment, I pulled him down to kiss him properly and to shut him up. He was right. Most people got together because they wanted to fuck and sometimes it turned into something more, and sometimes it didn't. I knew what Damian and I had was more than just lust, but worry niggled at the back of my mind because it didn't look like Billy Ray was going anywhere. How was this supposed to work out? I guessed we'd figure it out. We'd have to figure it out, or poof, the whole thing would blow up in our faces.

Epilogue

DAMIAN

"I think we should take the job in New Mexico. They have positions for all of us and sticking together is the only way we can stay safe." Billy Ray took a bite of her walleye, and then pointed her fork at me. "We can't keep living off your savings, and you know it."

"Yeah, you're not a millionaire, and the two of us can't keep mooching off you forever." Clay had a mouthful of fish, but that didn't stop him from adding his two cents.

"If you'd decide what you are going to do, we'd have more money." I was referring to him and his house, where he rarely stayed anymore but refused to admit he pretty much lived with me and Billy Ray. I wanted him to either move in with us full time, or for us to move to his house. I couldn't care less which one he chose if it meant I'd have him with me.

"My house isn't costing me that much, and I use my money to pay the bills on it." Clay was obstinate. It was true that he had some money also, but I had more and always insisted on paying for everything at my place so he could keep his.

"Do we really need to rehash this again?" Billy Ray was sick of the argument, but she never said what she'd prefer, instead, leaving the two of us to guess. "We need jobs. Let's stay on topic for once."

"So we go. I don't give a shit where it is as long as it's not Alabama again." Clay frowned. Our time in Alabama was a touchy subject for him on a couple of levels. All our nerves were worn thin waiting for my former pack to retaliate for the death of the leader's heir. So far all we'd heard was that the Luptons were deciding what they wanted from the Outcast pack to make reparations, but I was sure those vindictive assholes would do something to retaliate. It was just a matter of time, but with no insiders there, all we could do was wait.

"Is there room in the camper for all four of us?" Dante changed the subject because every time Alabama came up, he remembered that our parents were now hiding out in Tennessee, where Mom had a brother whose pack welcomed them, even with the mess they brought.

"The camper sleeps six so, yeah, there's room, but we might want to look in to putting my smaller camper onto your truck so you have a place that's more private." I loved my brother, but living with him at my place on the compound was hard enough when all four of us were there, being cooped up in a camper would probably end with one of us dead.

"Don't you think we should maybe think about which job is in the territory of the pack most likely not to want the three of us dead?"

"Most packs won't do shit." Dante's eyes shifted to Clay, who'd been the one to raise the issue, and then they widened. "Shit. How the hell are we supposed to travel with an infected?"

"Shut up, Dante." Billy Ray looked around to see if anyone was eavesdropping, but as usual on all-you-can-eat walleye night at the Pub, no one could give a shit about anything but the fish on their plates.

"We'll travel the same way we did last time. We'll decline to run with the pack and ask where we're free to do it on our own. Otherwise we'll stay out of trouble and out of their hair." I wasn't going to jeopardize any of us, and I knew what I was doing. "Besides, by the time we get something set up, Clay will be full grown. Since he can already sort of control his shifts, he shouldn't draw too much attention. It's Billy Ray I have to worry about now."

"Are we almost done here? I'd really like to get back to the compound before I shift."

"Then control it." Dante once again side-eyed Clay. I knew the two of them would come to blows eventually if they didn't have something to distract them. That was another reason why I was just as anxious to get back to work as Billy Ray was. It was a good thing our company had forgiven our running out on them. Kissing ass didn't suit any of us, but we'd done it so we could keep working at a place that paid so well.

"I'm anxious to get out and run, too, and I'm done eating." Billy Ray shifted in her chair. All three of us stopped chewing and sniffed the air. Her scent was still something that got our attention, which made her blush and look away. "There's our waitress." She lifted an arm to flag the woman down.

"I'll pay." I pulled out my wallet and gave the waitress my card. It was the same lady that was always there. Even though she knew Clay, Billy Ray, and I weren't interested in anything she had to offer, she still flirted with all of us.

Dante watched her walk off with my card before turning to Clay. "Are you sure I can't get her number?"

"You might be able to, but if you used it, her boyfriend, Hunter, would probably kill you." Clay threw his napkin on his plate and stood, followed by the rest of us.

I grabbed my card and receipt on our way out. I'd driven so we got in the truck to head back to the compound where we'd shift and run with the pack.

CLAY

The urge to shift still hit me hard, and I had to grit my teeth to stop it from just happening, which was why I wanted to leave the Pub before the time hit. The turnoff to the compound was coming up on the right so I just let go. I should have taken my clothes off first because now that I was bigger, my shirt and underwear didn't just land on top of me, they stayed on. It was uncomfortable but also the laughter of the other three in the truck when they saw me sitting there—a hundred-pound wolf wearing boxer briefs, a shirt, and a wolfy grin—was annoying.

"Shut up." Came out as a snarl, and when I asked one of them to take my damn shirt off, I used a series of barks punctuated with a low howl. I stood on the seat and the underwear fell off because they sat below my tail and had nothing holding them on, but the shirt was another story. I snapped at Billy Ray when he leaned over the seat from the back, but quickly changed my demeanor when I realized he was trying to help me while Damian, who was driving, and Dante just laughed at my predicament.

"I'll just pull this off for you." She grabbed my shirt and pulled it over my head. I licked her face to thank her for the help, making her grin before she sat back.

"That's the second time he's done that. I would have left him since he's too stupid to get naked before he shifts." Dante yelped when Billy Ray pinched his thigh for his mean words.

"He's still got a month before he's a yearling. I bet you couldn't even hold off the change for a couple of minutes before your wolf's first birthday." Billy Ray patted my head when I looked back to give Dante a look.

"I still think he's a moron." Dante sat with his arms crossed over his chest and stared out the window for the rest of our drive.

After Damian parked, I hopped out his door and promptly started chasing my tail because that's the way things went when my beast was let out of its cage.

"See, complete moron, still chasing his tail." Dante went past me and up the stairs to the house. "I'm going to meet with a few friends. Catch you guys later." He left us standing in the driveway.

"I hope he's not getting mixed up with people who are going to get him in trouble." Damian bent to scratch me behind the ears. "Let's go to Pete and Willard's and see if they need any help with stuff before we shift for the night."

Billy Ray nodded and followed while I ran ahead. They passed me as I stopped to drink out of a mud puddle, and then I bounded ahead of them. It went that way for the entire walk to the pack leader's house because my bouncy ball puppy brain found nature way more interesting than my human brain did.

Pete and Willard were in the yard directing families with children and pups to the nursery while fist bumping the teenage werewolves as they passed into the fenced-in area for some training that Willard and Pete would oversee before they joined the pack on the run. I'd been a part of that group for a time so I went to greet a couple of the guys I knew who knelt and gave me scratches after I'd sniffed their crotches and/or asses, ignoring Damian as he chatted with Willard.

When Billy Ray caught my attention, I turned and jumped up on her, my paws landing on her chest. "You're being a bad puppy, aren't you?" Her big grin didn't match her words. When I licked her face, she giggled, which drew Pete's eyes to us.

Pete bent his head in close to Willard, and then they both looked at Billy Ray as they scented the air. Willard whispered something to Damian who frowned, and that's when I lost the thread because someone had a donut. I dropped down to all fours and followed my nose to the woman who had a bag of those little bite-sized powdered-sugar ones. I sat and gave her my best puppy dog eyes—easy since I was a dog—and she threw one up in the air. Swallowing, after only pretending to chew, I was about to beg for another when Damian called my name.

"Clay." He saw my hesitation to leave the almost full bag of donuts behind and put a little more energy behind the call. I loped over to him and could smell the tension in the air as he and Billy Ray stood close together. "We're going to go run somewhere a little different tonight so stay with me and Billy Ray when we shift."

I gave one sharp bark to let him know I'd understood what he was saying and then followed them back down the road where Damian took a turn and led us down a smaller lane and into the trees. Sniffing around, I ignored the two of them as they undressed and shifted, but then my nose caught a scent that made my beast turn and run headlong into Billy Ray.

BILLY RAY

Knowing Clay was barely out of the puppy stage did nothing to stop me from snapping and snarling at him when he wouldn't get his nose out of my ass. It took Damian coming over and shouldering Clay away from me to make him stop, and he still tried to do it again. Damian's wolf was a bit bigger than Clay's, but Clay had more power, even though he wasn't quite full grown, and Damian ended up standing between us, growling at him.

Clay plopped down on his hind end and stared at me with his tongue lolling out of his mouth. He cocked his head and narrowed his eyes in an entirely too human expression. Seconds later, he changed forms and stood up. I didn't understand his words in the way I would have if I'd been human, but his tone told me he was upset about something so I shifted at the same time as Damian.

"Okay, one of you better fucking explain what the hell is going on with Billy Ray's wolf." He put his hands on his slim waist, which drew my eyes to his cock, and I had to quickly turn away before he caught me eyeballing his junk.

"What are you babbling about?" Damian didn't look happy about having to shift two times so closely together.

"Tell me why we're not running with the pack." Clay glared at me, probably figuring it was my fault, and he was right.

"I can't be around the other wolves when I'm in my female form." It was that simple. Being an omega meant that most of the other male wolves would be driven to try to claim me, and the only way to do that was to mate with me.

"Okay, that answers one question. Now tell me how the fuck your wolf is all of a sudden female when I've seen you as a male wolf all the other times."

"He's bigendered. He told you that." Damian looked at Clay like he was just playing dumb, but I could see the real confusion there and took pity on him.

"I've been feminine all day, which you know because you've used the proper pronouns." I hit the one thing that made him smile because he remembered the first time we'd talked about it. "My wolf matches the gender I am, so sometimes my wolf is male and sometimes, like tonight, it's female."

Clay's jaw dropped down as he stared at me, but then he seemed to get control of himself. "So, you really do have two genders." He said the words in a way that made me bristle. Did he think I was making it up?

"Well, duh. You can smell the difference on her when she's one or the other." Damian was adding nothing to the discussion, and I was starting to get a little annoyed with both of them.

"Are we done now? I'd like to shift and make the most of what's left of the night."

Clay shook his head. "I'm still not sure I understand what this all means."

"It means she needs extra protection when she's in her wolf form. That should be all you need to know." Damian took a protective step in my direction, but I held up a hand to stop him.

"That's not all it means, but maybe we can discuss all the other things some other time. Like when we're not standing around naked when it's barely fifty degrees out."

"Okay, fine, but I want some answers later." Clay shifted back into his wolf form, making me wonder how hard it had been for him to do all that shifting. It also drove home just how powerful the infecteds were.

"I'm not even sure of all the things it means." Damian gave me a look, and then he too shifted, leaving me standing there.

Those two were going to be the death of me, I thought as I shifted, and then forgot everything except the feeling of the ground under my paws and the wind in my fur.

Acknowledgements

I know this part is getting stale but without Tonna Saunders, Jamila Lindsey, and Christina Quinn, none of my books would ever get written, so thanks, ladies, for having my back. And to Barb, for once again putting up with my whining during the editing process.

About the Author

CL Mustafic is a born and bred American Midwesterner who mysteriously ended up living in a tiny Eastern European country. Left with too much time on her hands—let's be honest here, it was the lack of television channels in her native language—and too many voices in her head trying to fill the silence, she decided to give her lifelong dream of writing a novel a shot. So now between shuttling kids back and forth from various activities, risking her life on the insanely narrow, busy streets of her new hometown, she loses herself in her own made-up world where love always wins.

Website: www.clmustafic.com

Facebook: www.facebook.com/clmustafic.author

Twitter: @CL_Mustafic

Other books by this author

Loving Sarajevo
Falling for Him
Glory Hole to Hell
Christmas Cookies
"Satin Secrets" within *Beneath the Layers*

Outcasts Series

Bad Moon Arising

Also Available from NineStar Press

Connect with NineStar Press

Website: NineStarPress.com

Facebook: NineStarPress

Facebook Reader Group: NineStarNiche

Twitter: @ninestarpress

Tumblr: NineStarPress